Fiction

M

Celebration in
the Northwest

Celebration in the Northwest

ANA MARÍA MATUTE

Fiesta al Noroeste
Translated by Phoebe Ann Porter

University of Nebraska Press, Lincoln and London

Originally published as *Fiesta al
Noroeste*, Copyright Ediciones
Destino S.A., Barcelona, 1963.
This edition has been translated
with financial assistance of the
Spanish Dirección General del
Libro y Bibliotecas of the
Ministerio de Cultura.
Translation © 1997 by the
University of Nebraska Press.
Library of Congress Cataloging-
in-Publication Data. Matute,
Ana María, 1926– [Fiesta al
noroeste. English] Celebration
in the Northwest / Ana María
Matute; translated by Phoebe
Ann Porter.   p. cm. –
(European women writers series)
ISBN 0-8032-3180-6 (cl : alk.
paper)   ISBN 0-8032-8196-x (pbk.).
I. Porter, Phoebe Ann.
II. Title.   III. Series.
PQ6623.A89F513   1997
863'.64 – dc20   96-18583 CIP

Contents

Translator's Introduction

Ana María Matute is not only one of Spain's most important novelists of the post–civil war period (1939 to present) but also one of its most prolific writers of this century. Since 1948 she has published, in addition to numerous articles in periodicals, some twenty-eight volumes: ten novels; ten collections of stories, essays, and sketches; and eight books for children. Her works have been translated into at least twenty-three languages, including German, French, Japanese, Russian, Dutch, and Swedish. Four of her novels and one collection of stories have been translated into English.[1] She has received Spain's most prestigious literary awards, including the Café Gijón Prize in 1952 for *Fiesta al Noroeste* (*Celebration in the Northwest*); the Planeta Prize, 1954, for *Pequeño teatro* (Little theater); the National Literature Prize, 1959, for *Los hijos muertos* (*The Lost Children*); and the Nadal Prize, 1959, for *Primera memoria* (*School of the Sun*); as well as many awards for her works for children. She has spoken on literature at universities throughout Europe and has been a visiting lecturer and resident writer at three universities in the United States: Indiana (1965), Oklahoma (1969), and Virginia (1978). Matute's reading public in the United States has grown through frequent classroom use of her novels and stories.

A precocious child, Matute began writing at an early age as an escape. She explains: "When I was a child and the world rejected me, I began to write in order to invent a world for myself. And I continue doing it. It is a way of being in the world. Writing is living, living in a world that I have invented for myself."[2] Nevertheless, for Matute, literature is not only a refuge but a protest against injustice in the world around her, a condemnation of authoritarian social order, and a personal response to the inevitable disillusionments of life. Her fiction for adults is usually classified as social realism, yet her language is highly poetic and subjective.

Matute was born in Barcelona in 1926, the daughter of a Catalan industrialist. She had the Catholic upbringing traditional for girls of her social class. Her education was often interrupted by childhood illnesses and long, lonely periods of convalescence during which she voraciously devoured children's literature: *Alice in Wonderland, Peter Pan,* and fairy tales by Hans Christian Andersen and the brothers Grimm. She began writing stories, which she illustrated, and plays for a puppet theater. The days that she spent alone created in her a sense of loneliness and alienation that many of her fictional characters experience.

Matute recovered from sickness and spent summer vacations at her maternal grandparents' home in the small mountain village of Mansilla de la Sierra in the Rioja region of northern Spain. There, she observed a side of life very different from her own sheltered existence in a comfortable middle-class family. In the village she witnessed the degrading poverty of the Castilian country people and the hardships they endured. She was a sensitive and observant child; her lengthy stays in the countryside left a lasting impression and provided material for many of her works. In her memoirs, *El río* (The river, 1972), she records lyric descriptions of scenes from village life. The fictitious village of Artámila, setting of *Celebration in the Northwest* and the stories of *Historias de la Artámila* (Tales of Artámila), is based directly on her observations of rural life in Mansilla de la Sierra, where in the early 1930s Castilian laborers lived as landless serfs working the fields of wealthy landlords.

viii

Shortly before Matute's tenth birthday, in July of 1936, the Spanish civil war broke out. The three terrible years of strife that tore her country apart and the wretched postwar years were crucial to her development as a writer, as they were to all those of her generation. Her family spent the duration of the war in the Republican zone of Barcelona, an area agitated by anarcho-syndicalism and other leftist labor movements. Matute witnessed the bloody social revolution, bombings, terror, and death in Barcelona's streets. On a personal level, the war marked the end of her childhood and, without doubt, helped to form the pessimistic vision evident in all of her works for adults. The loss of childhood innocence and security, the death of illusions, the betrayal of friends, and the strife between brothers — these constant themes in Matute's fiction reflect the savagery of the civil war and the suffering and disillusionment of the postwar "years of hunger," as Spaniards refer to the forties.

The Franco regime was established in 1939 and lasted more than three decades. With its police-state atmosphere, persecution of political enemies and intellectuals, and censorship of the arts, it stifled the writers of Matute's generation; they had to learn to write between the lines in order to express their real views. Matute says that "the writer became conditioned, completely and thoroughly, by this artifice called censorship whose worst and greatest damage is the habit of self-censorship which it created in authors. . . . The writer, especially if he is a beginner, through fear, and because of his natural desire to have his works published, ends up being the worst censor of his own works."[3]

Strict censorship made direct criticism of church or state impossible. Matute was forced to take an indirect approach to subjects such as the civil war, social injustice, and the role of the Spanish Church. Often, she resorted to archetypal imagery. For example, the biblical motif of Cain and Abel, found throughout her work and particularly relevant to the novel *Celebration in the Northwest,* addresses questions of fraternal conflict and fratricide. Matute observes: "In the world there are only three or four themes and one of them is Cain and Abel, perhaps the most powerful."[4]

Cain saw that Abel was his most beautiful image in the world, what he would have liked to appear to others. And he knew that Abel was going to grow and to be greater than others. At the same time, he was envious, profoundly envious of him. Not the petty, mediocre envy of he's got it and I want it. No, it was the envy of God, the hunger and thirst for God. God won't accept my sacrifices, but accepts those of Abel because Abel is my most beautiful image. He felt such a great love for Abel that it turned into hatred. And he killed his most beautiful image because he knew that if he didn't kill him, disillusionment and old age would kill him. And he told himself, "Abel will always be a beautiful child whose sacrifices God will accept." And then he killed Abel – this is my own theory – so that he would not turn into Cain. Because Cain was the first child in the world, and the first child in the world is a murderer. All children in the world murder their most beautiful image – childhood.[5]

Matute's theory about Cain and Abel helps to shed light on the complex and, at times, seemingly contradictory relationships between the characters of her novels. For Matute, the Cain and Abel story is more than a myth of sibling rivalry: it is the story of the fight between childhood and adulthood, Abel representing the beauty and innocence of childhood and Cain, the adolescent, struggling between childhood and adulthood.

Although Matute considers her first published novel, *Los Abel* (The Abel family, 1948), to be her worst, it is significant in terms of her overall work in that it presents for the first time the Cain and Abel motif that she reworked in *Celebration in the Northwest, Tres fantasías y un sueño* (Three fantasies and a dream), *The Lost Children,* and *School of the Sun.* She is prouder of her second published novel, *Celebration in the Northwest* (1952). In the prologue to her collected works, she points out that *Celebration* contains a "premeditated and ordered protest" against "an expiring world in the face of another trying to survive beneath a shower of sterilizing myths."[6] In this novel she sought to expose the falseness of the Spanish myths of good-natured paternalism, Christian charity, even-handed justice, piety and devotion, nobility, honor, and so forth.[7] She says that the characters turned into symbols on their own: "Pablo incarnates the stubborn will to live, to free himself from all that has been imposed upon him; his brother Juan, on the other hand, is immobility, the weight of power sunk in the most inane apathy and uselessness."[8] The confrontation between traditional order and hope for a new world lies at the heart of the story, which can be read as an allegory of the two Spains that came into conflict during the Spanish civil war.

In *Celebration in the Northwest,* Matute criticizes the almost medieval social order of the Spanish countryside that she witnessed as a child in Mansilla de la Sierra. Juan Medinao, the protagonist, represents the class of powerful rural landowners who virtually own their laborers. Throughout the novel we sense Matute's compassion for the poor and oppressed, whose lives she describes with realism and tenderness.

Spanish religiosity also comes under scrutiny. Because of strict censorship, criticism of the church could never be direct, yet here it is clearly implied. Matute subtly exposes the hypocrisy of a church that claims to champion the meek yet supports the rich and powerful. The character of Juan Medinao, who uses religion as a social mask, embodies false piety. The portrayal of religious instruction by the clergy reflects the author's dissatisfaction with her own Catholic education. In the protagonist's spiritual development, we see the gradual perversion and eventual corruption of the pure love of God that he felt as a child.

The first chapter of the novel, which centers on Dingo the puppeteer, introduces themes that will be developed later on: the impossibility of escaping from miserable reality into fantasy, the death of childhood, and loss of youthful illusions. Like the protagonist, Dingo can never escape his childhood memories, try as he may. Disillusionment and moral degradation characterize his adult life. Behind his cheerful masks and the fantasy world he has created lurk miserable reality and death.

Despite its brevity, *Celebration* is a fairly complex work. It tells two stories separated by over thirty years: the accidental death and burial of the shepherd's child in the narrative present, and Juan Medinao's childhood reconstructed retrospectively through the device of confession. Plot is subordinated to the development of the protagonist's personality. Relationships between characters are complicated, involving the Cain and Abel conflict between brothers, with elements of incestuous homosexuality, and the Oedipal conflict between Juan and his father, whose mistress, Salome, is the mother of Juan's half-brother. Biblical allusions and religious motifs appear throughout. Margaret Jones comments: "Matute uses religious practices to best novelistic advantage. The confession as a framework for Juan's story ironically underscores the unchristian basis of his fanatical devotion."[9]

Celebration contains most of Matute's characteristic stylistic traits, such as strikingly original imagery. Repetition, synaesthesia, personification, and oxymoron create a lyrical style not to be mistaken for that of any other contemporary Spanish novelist. Color symbolism, especially the dramatic contrast of black, white, and red, is evident throughout the work. Her use of color to express concepts and emotions has earned Matute frequent comparisons to the dark and dramatic paintings of the Spanish expressionist José Gutiérrez Solana. The harsh climate and stark scenery of the novel evoke moods of solitude, gloom, and fear. Images relating to nature and the senses, instead of being strictly realistic, lyrically suggest the state of mind of the central character. The cycles of nature in the Castilian countryside, such as the sowing and harvesting of wheat, also relate thematically to the lives of the characters.

In 1952, the same year that *Celebration* won the prestigious Café Gijón prize, Matute married the novelist Ramón Eugenio de Goicoechea. Although the marriage proved unhappy and resulted in sep-

aration in 1963, the birth of their son, Juan Pablo, in 1954 was a sin-
gularly joyful event in Matute's life. A mother deeply involved in her
child's world, she began writing books for children. Since 1956, she
has produced eight works of juvenile fiction and has translated tales
by Aesop, Mark Twain, Hans Christian Andersen, and the brothers
Grimm, thus notably enriching Spanish children's literature.

The additional financial responsibilities that accompanied the
birth of Juan Pablo forced Matute to rewrite a novel about the civil
war, *Luciérnagas* (Fireflies, 1953), that had been censored because it
presented neither Franco's National Movement nor the Spanish
Church in a positive light. Matute hated the rewritten version, published in 1955 under the title *En esta tierra* (In this land), and felt
ashamed for having had to sacrifice her principles for economic reasons: "Needless to say, this abortion meant and still means for me an
abandonment of principles that is hard to swallow."[10] In 1993, forty
years after its creation and nearly two decades after Franco's death, a
new, carefully revised *Luciérnagas* appeared in print. Centering on
the experience of young people in Barcelona whose idealism and
lives are shattered during the civil war, the novel should help keep
alive in the Spanish collective memory the horrors of that dreadful
conflict.

Between 1951 and 1958, Matute worked on *Los hijos muertos (The
Lost Children)*, a monumental novel over five hundred pages long,
considered by many to be her masterpiece. Like *Luciérnagas*, this
work is also based on the lives of young people during the civil war,
but it differs from the earlier novel in that it is set in a small village in
conservative and nationalist Old Castile. *Los hijos muertos* presents a
panoramic view of several generations of a family and a wide cross-
section of Spanish society, and rather than the social causes of the
war, it analyzes the war's effect on individuals. Although the author
strives to remain nonpartisan in her presentation, in this as in all of
her work, we sense more sympathy for the losers of the war than for
its winners.

Los hijos muertos won two important literary awards: the Critic's Prize in 1958 and the National Prize for Literature in 1959. The novel garnered such critical acclaim that in 1959 Matute received a substantial grant to work on her trilogy about the Spanish civil war, *Los mercaderes* (The merchants). The following year she produced the first volume of the trilogy, *Primera memoria* (translated as both *School of the Sun* and *The Awakening*). Narrated from the perspective of an adolescent girl, this novel incorporates many of Matute's constant themes: the Cain and Abel conflict, social injustice, the loss of youthful idealism, and the gap between childhood and adulthood. It does not focus directly on the war, which is taking place on the Iberian Peninsula; rather, it centers on the lives of children from various classes in Mallorca who only hear of the war as a distant echo. In this story of a girl's passage into adulthood, with its inevitable compromise and corruption, Matute concentrates on the underlying social and personal causes of war. Its themes and lyrical style make *Primera memoria* one of Matute's most significant and characteristic novels.

The last two volumes of the trilogy appeared some years later: *Los soldados lloran de noche* (Soldiers cry at night) in 1964 and *La trampa* (The trap) in 1969. The second volume takes place during the closing months of the war and centers on the solitude and confusion of the soldiers who are fighting a war of the merchant class. The third volume experiments with a complicated narrative structure that incorporates four intertwining perspectives. As it is in most of Matute's fiction, plot is secondary to character study in *La trampa*, which explores the lives of the four narrators, two of whom are principal characters of *Primera memoria*. Themes of this last novel of the trilogy include the aftereffects of the war, personal revenge, and the decadence of a family.

Since the late 1960s, Matute's literary production has slowed down considerably. Her fantastic novel, *La torre vigía* (The watch tower, 1971), one of her most original creations, takes place during the Middle Ages and tells the story of a young knight's apprenticeship. Although the setting is radically different from that of her earlier works, the social conflicts presented in *La torre vigía* are similar to those of *Celebration in the Northwest*. In both novels, landless peasants are brutalized by a decadent aristocracy, and the elemental forces of violence, envy, betrayal, and sexual desire move the characters. Natural imagery (sun, land, and wind) and color symbolism (black, white, and red) also play an important role.

Matute is also one of Spain's best writers of short fiction. Since 1956 she has produced ten collections of stories, essays, and literary sketches in which children figure significantly. *Los niños tontos* (The foolish children, 1956), a collection of lyrical vignettes about children's fantasy world and its clash with reality, is considered by Camilo José Cela, Spain's latest Nobel Prize laureate (1989), to be "the most important work written in Spanish by a woman since the Countess Emilia Pardo Bazán."[11] Other outstanding collections of stories include: *El tiempo* (Time, 1957), in which many stories focus on children; *Historias de la Artámila* (Tales from Artámila, 1961), which centers on the difficult lives of Castilian country people; *El arrepentido* (The repentant one, 1961), which has no unifying theme; and *Algunos muchachos*, which appeared in 1968 and has recently been translated into English by Michael Scott Doyle as *The Heliotrope Wall and Other Stories* (1989). Matute's latest collection of stories, *La virgen de Antioquía y otros relatos* (The virgin of Antioquía and other stories, 1990), contains one new story but otherwise consists of reprinted stories from *El arrepentido*.

Ana María Matute may be ranked, along with Camilo José Cela and Miguel Delibes, among Spain's most distinguished writers of fiction in this century. What sets her apart from many of her contemporaries who strive for objective realism is her lyrical, subjective discourse. Her work ranges from delightful fantasies written for children to realistic adult narratives based on her own wartime and postwar experiences dealing with the trials of growing up, the civil war, social injustice, and the life of Spanish peasants. Her treatment of childhood and adolescence is especially sensitive without being sentimental. Her vision of adulthood is decidedly pessimistic, for it involves the compromise of principles and the betrayal of youthful idealism. A mood of sorrow and disillusionment often pervades her writing. Although she never advocates a particular ideology in her fiction, her sympathies most clearly lie with the innocent, the outcast, the unfortunate, the oppressed, and the vanquished.

Notes

1 *Los hijos muertos* has been translated by Joan MacLean as *The Lost Children* (New York: Macmillan, 1963). *Primera memoria* has been translated by both James H. Mason, as *Awakening* (New York: Hutchison, 1963) and Elaine Kerrigan, as *School of the Sun* (New York: Pantheon, 1963; New York: Columbia University Press, 1989). The story collection *Algunos muchachos* has been translated by Michael S. Doyle, as *The Heliotrope Wall and Other Stories* (New York: Columbia University Press, 1989).

2 Ana María Matute, "Entrevista con Ana María Matute: 'Recuperar otra vez cierta inocencia,'" interview by Michael Scott Doyle, *Anales de la literatura española contemporánea* 10 (1985): 238. My translation.

3 Ana María Matute, "Prologue," in *Obra completa*, vol. 2 (Barcelona: Destino, 1975), 7.

4 Matute, "Entrevista," 238. My translation.

5 Matute, "Entrevista," 245. My translation.

6 Ana María Matute, "Prologue," in *Obra completa*, vol. 1 (Barcelona: Destino, 1971), 21.

7 Matute, "Prologue," 1:21.

8 Matute, "Prologue," 1:22.

9 Margaret Jones, *The Literary World of Ana María Matute* (Lexington: University Press of Kentucky, 1970), 8.

10 Matute, "Prologue," 2:10.

11 Cela in Janet Díaz, *Ana María Matute* (Boston: Twayne, 1977), 77. Margaret Jones's book and Díaz's study are the most comprehensive examinations in English of Matute's life and work. Emilia Pardo Bazán (1851–1921), to whom Cela compares Matute, is widely considered Spain's most important woman writer and intellectual. Pardo Bazán wrote some twenty long novels, twenty novellas, over six hundred short stories, and numerous works of literary criticism.

Celebration in
the Northwest

1

Dingo cracked his whip crisply, like a streak of black lightning. It had been raining since dawn; now it was nearly six in the afternoon, three days before Ash Wednesday. Water soaked the old horse's mane as the puppeteer's wagon trundled along mumbling its myriad burnt-out noises: trained dogs yawning, wigged masks smiling, and long, long voiceless laments.

Dingo, in the driver's seat, felt all this like a tickle on the nape of his neck. Behind him, within the cart painted in seven colors, lay the old trunk full of costumes, his deaf-mute brother who played the drum, and three trained dogs, all asleep beneath the patter of the rain.

They had just entered the Artámila region and, in full carnival spirit, were crossing the helpless land. Artámila, with its hostile soil and sky, hardly rewarded man's labor. The town consisted of three villages: Upper, Lower, and Central Artámila. In the last of these, also called Greater Artámila, were to be found the town hall and the parish church. From Lower Artámila, the poorest village, which now came into view in the depths of the valley, Dingo had escaped as a young boy, chasing after a troupe of acrobats. Dingo, whose real name was Domingo, was born on a Sunday and sought to make his life a perpetual holiday. Now, after all those years, or hours – who could tell the difference? – his own actor's wagon stopped precisely on the edge of the steep ridge, above the wide road that, like inevitable destiny, descended to the first of the three villages. A precipitous and violent road, made only to swallow you up.

With a pained look, his eyes recoiling from the scene below, Dingo saw the valley again, after such a long time. How deep it appeared, framed by brown-colored rocks. How deep, with its miserable hovels half-erased by the dirty fingers of hunger. There they were again, the oak forests on the hillsides, the proud, tapering, green poplars. In groups, and yet, each tree breathing its own arrogant solitude, like the men of that valley. Those men from Artámila, with dark skin and big hands. On the driver's seat of the stalled wagon, Dingo remained motionless, his arm raised, ready to whip on the horse. His eyes were set wide apart. It was as if he went through the world with his eyes on his temples so that he would not have to see life straight on. On the edges of his raincoat hood, on the hubs of the wheels, raindrops tinkled frozen sparks. Dingo spat and lashed the horse.

Then the whole cart whined, every board, one by one. Down the slope he rushed, hoping to run Artámila through like a sword, disdainful of old offenses he was sorry he had not forgotten. He would escape and once more climb to the summit in front of him, on the other side of the valley, leaving behind forever the red pool of the village under its rain and implacable skies. The cartwheels, inconsiderately yoked together like any human couple, were already red from the mud, and they screeched through every patch, each with different complaints. At that moment, Dingo felt he carried the weight of those wheels fastened to the ribs of his own body.

The dogs began to bark, falling into a heap within the wagon, and for a moment Dingo took pleasure in imagining the masks' smiles losing their stiffness under the wigs.

A bolt of lightning turned the earth white. He had to hurry through Artámila, where people didn't care for dramas written in verse anyway. On the other side, once he had reached the blue mountains in the distance, Dingo could go back to dragging along his merrymaking, his pantomimes with ten characters represented by a single second-rate actor. He, and he alone, with ten different masks, ten voices, and ten different reasons. The deaf-mute's drum would sound again, like a prayer in a cave. The deaf-mute and the three dogs, their rib cages trembling under the lash, would wait for their beating and their bread on the other side of the puppeteer's smile. Dingo was well aware that his miserable companions would eventually die, perhaps one by one, in the gutters or against lamp-posts along the road. When that day came, he and his ten phantoms would go on roaming the world alone, earning the daily bread and indispensable wine. What a day that would be when, alone, with his trunk full of golden cords stolen from the village sacristies, he would go down the road with his ten voices and his ten reasons for living. He assumed that they would always let him through, always. Entitled, in the end, to ten deaths, upon turning the corners.

Meanwhile, the wagon, an enormous seven-colored smile splattered with mud, dragged along its parodies and maybe as well all those events that had done so much harm long ago.

It is possible that Dingo might have seen the child as he popped up suddenly at a bend in the road. A scrawny little figure, quite the opposite of Dingo himself, he unexpectedly came into view. What is certain is that he could not have avoided running him over. Without intending to, Dingo bore down upon the child with all of his old and badly painted life.

The clouds were dark overhead. He braked as best he could, doubling over amid the groaning of the cart. Splashes of muddy slime spotted his beard, seeking out his swearing mouth. Dingo could feel the tender and fresh crunching of bones under the wheels.

Then, silence fell around them. It was as if a wide and open hand reached down from the sky to flatten him once and for all against the very ground he so wanted to flee. What is more, he had known it all along. Inner voices had warned him: "You will not make it through Artámila." He had just run over one of those children who take food

3

out to their shepherd fathers. A few yards farther on lay the little open basket, scattering its silent desperation under the downpour.

All that was screaming before – wind, axles, dogs – was now silent, piercing him with a hundred eyes of sharpened iron. Cursing, he jumped down and sank into the mud up to his ankles. Then he saw him: a child dressed in gray, wearing only one canvas sandal. He was very quiet now, as if surprised by poppies.

Still holding his whip high, Dingo could not help yelling at him. But almost immediately the curses died in his throat. He crouched down, quietly, drilled through by eyes, by silence, by the distant arrogance of the poplars that were staring at him from the hillside. Dingo tried to speak to that motionless, scrawny little face. The rain continued drizzling down indifferently. It fell across the child's forehead in shiny threads, on his eyelashes and closed lips. At that moment, Dingo thought he saw the clouds reflected in the child's eyes. They crossed over them slowly and went off toward other lands.

Half an hour of road remained ahead to the village. The dogs and the deaf-mute peered out of the windows of the cart. Their wet noses trembled, and their glassy yellow eyes watched him steadily. Dingo put both hands around the back of the child. He linked his wide fingers together in the mud and lifted the small body, feeling that it might break in two. He noted a lukewarm stickiness on the skin. The dogs began to howl. Dingo looked at them timidly.

"He has broken. . . ," he began to say. But the deaf-mute, a string of saliva hanging from his lip, did not understand him. And the child's eyes were now definitively black.

Against his will, Dingo looked down toward one end of the town: there in the distance, at the base of the mountain, was a square of reddish dirt, surrounded by a wall riddled with cracks. It was the Northwest Cemetery, with its fallen crosses, where the men of Artámila hid their dead. Once, someone had planted next to the wall a row of twelve poplars, which had grown into a black and empty smile, like the teeth of a comb.

4

Dingo hesitated. He could still leave the child on the ground and gallop through the town without stopping, until he reached a land without burdensome memories for him, without rotten dreams, without his own blood. He could probably get there before the sun came up. The deaf-mute and the dogs had jumped out of the wagon and stood around him expectantly.

Then, the deaf-mute shuddered with fear. Poor fool, his soul was infected by pantomimes. Rolling his eyes, he emitted a hoarse noise and began to gesticulate: "Boy dead," he mimed, "Dead . . . They'll hang you from a post." And he stuck out his tongue. The child's body weighed heavily in Dingo's arms. "They'll hang you and they'll . . ." The idiot jumped up suddenly, with open arms, and fell to the ground. He was carrying the drum around his neck, and when he fell it resonated for a long while: as if it held in its belly the voice its owner never had.

Without a doubt, it was the sound of the drum that startled the old horse. But Dingo was already inclined to believe that it was the evil spirit of Artámila, the evil spirit that had embittered his childhood and, ever since that morning when he set foot again on the soil of his homeland, welcomed him with malicious faces.

He felt cold. He pressed the bloody body against his own. Maybe it was the evil spirit that pushed the wagon with its crazed horse downhill. Not even Dingo had time to yell anything. He saw his wagon rushing headlong, without brakes or control this time, its ramshackle awning trembling dangerously and the little scarlet curtains waving a desperate farewell. The steep slope led into the central plaza of Lower Artámila. The wagon did not stop. It would not stop until it had reached the heart of the village, surrounded by brown houses and high hills. Dingo saw it disappear into the depths, rattling apart, swallowed by the throat of the valley. He stood there quietly among the dogs, his beard soaked by the storm, his boots sunk deep in the mud.

For a while he remained so, struggling with himself. But he gave

5

up. Artámila was waiting below, as deep and black as he carried it in his soul.

The sky had darkened even more when he began his descent with the boy in his arms. The three dogs followed, and a little farther back, the deaf-mute, drum hanging from his neck, stumbled over the stones with the puffed-up seriousness of a bird of evil omen. They went down in a row, like the poplars. Under the rain. Without light.

There was the village plaza that Dingo knew so well: a circle of hard-packed dirt, red as blood.

The puppeteer stopped on its edge, wearing almost the same fearful expression as the houses crowded around the plaza. There was something tragic there, as there is in every heart. He was in the very center of Artámila, in the deepest part of the valley. How the wind used to speak to Dingo, up there on the mountaintops. As to an equal. But now he was plunged back into the truth, without a mask. There he was again, as if no time had passed. Swallowed up by that land, naked, and completely alone. The party had died for him in one blow.

He looked up and around, almost ashamed of his desire for freedom. Once again the mountains seemed to grow in their colossal disdain. There he was, a man with ten lies, with little he could do about it. His ten reasons fell to the ground, and he just stood there like a black tree whipped by the cold. In those same woods he knew so well, his childhood had been buried, bit by bit. He remembered himself as a boy, skirting the trees, perhaps limping from a thorn that had pierced his foot. How useless everything turns out in the end. Those who fled, those who stayed behind, those who painted their faces – oh, if only back then, when he was still a barefoot boy, a colorful wagon had run him over. . . ! If only the red soil had embraced him, had embraced his sides, his forehead, and his thirsty mouth. Maybe the child that he now carried in his arms was himself. How could he

6

evade his own funeral. . . ? No one. No one can. "The children who don't die, where are they now?" Here, then, was his landscape: unchanged and hard, surrounding all of his disguises, mocking his seven colors.

In the center of the plaza lay the wagon, fallen on its side, broken to pieces, with one wheel detached. The horse, probably lame, lay on the ground as well, his legs folded beneath him and his mouth foaming in the rain. The animal's eyes like moons were watching him; he may have been crying inaudibly. The little dead body grew heavier and heavier in Dingo's arms.

Through the windows of the wagon came a hullabaloo like that of rooks on their first flight. Dingo then realized that the village children had assaulted what was left of his house on wheels. All the village children. "Those children of Artámila who appear unexpectedly, quietly turning the sharp corner, without shoes or belts." Even with his eyes closed, Dingo could see them running around the corners of the workmen's huts. The children of Artámila, under the moon, with their long shadows and their short names. Just as he might have come around the corner of his house back then: feeling the fire of the earth underfoot and evoking far away, tangled in the tops of the poplars, the false echo of a bell heard a year before when they took him to the parish church for communion. The church was in Central Artámila, eight kilometers from his village; the children of Lower Artámila grew up without bells. Dingo stared into the face of his broken child. The same. Everything the same. Thirty years may have passed, but they were the same children, with the same footsteps and the same thirst. The same miserable houses, the same tilled land under the sky, the same death in the Northwest Cemetery. Thirty years, all for what. . . ? "The children of Artámila, children without toys, who snicker behind their hands and go down to the river to drown unwanted kittens." When he was very little, Dingo had made himself a mask of clay, sticking it to his face until the sun dried it; during the night it had fallen to pieces.

Now, for the children of Artámila, a whirlwind of color had fallen down the slope and crashed there in the very heart of their lives. They had approached it, little by little, one by one. They had watched, in the endless silence of the village, how the great red wheel flew off. They saw it roll and roll toward the river, toward the ghosts of drowned dogs and cats. But, halfway there, the wheel gave up, falling onto its hub, and remained spinning, and spinning, each time more slowly.

"I have no other choice," Dingo said to himself. "I have to look up Juan Medinao . . ."

Just like thirty years before.

2

His name was Juan Medinao, like his father and his father's father before him. Usury, practiced formerly by his grandfather, had turned him into the nearly absolute owner of Lower Artámila. Since he had come of age, it was apparent that he was the owner and master of something he had not earned. The house and lands were too big for him, especially the house. He called it the house of the Juans, and it was ugly, with three large plots of dark crimson earth and a central patio of flagstones. At nightfall, the windows were red; at dawn, navy blue. The house was located some distance from the village, directly opposite the Northwest Cemetery. From his bedroom window, Juan Medinao could watch all the burials.

That Shrove Sunday, as evening was coming on, Juan Medinao was praying. Since childhood he had known that these were days of atonement and holy amends. Perhaps his prayer was an inventory, the sum and balance of all the daily humiliations to which he had exposed his heart. There he was in the dark, the fire in the hearth dying, with his two hands intertwined like roots.

Night had entered the house, and rain whipped incessantly against the balcony. When it rained like that, Juan Medinao felt the throbbing of the water on the windowpanes almost physically, like a desperate drumbeat.

He heard them calling him. Human voices drilled through the

thin wall and jolted him from his spiritual revery. They continued calling him. Everyone in the house, down to the lowest houseboy, knew that Juan Medinao prayed during those hours and that he should not be interrupted. But they kept it up. His heart burst with anger. He shouted and threw his shoe at the door.

"Open the door, Juan Medinao!" they shouted. "It's the constable. He's here with a policeman from the detachment . . ."

Juan stared at his shoe on the floor, his deformed mouth gaping. He felt terribly alienated from the walls, the floor, the ceiling. It was as if the entire room spat him toward God. He stood up and slid back the bolt. A maid was there, with her hands hidden under her apron.

"I'm coming," he said. Immediately he regretted his tone of voice. He tried to correct it by explaining gently: "You interrupted me, I was surrounded by angels . . ."

The girl lowered her head, and covering her mouth, she ran downstairs ahead of him. Juan Medinao inspired either fear or laughter in young girls.

Slowly he descended the stairs. The drawing room was dark.

"What's going on?" he said. In the dim light, the men loomed as blackish hulks. Their faces, lighter, seemed to float in the air. The policeman explained that he had detained a juggler for running over Pedro Cruz's son. It was an accident; his wagon had ended up a wreck in the middle of the plaza. This clown was asking Juan Medinao for help.

"What does he want from me?"

The constable and the policeman did not answer.

"I'll go," he said. He approached the window, peered through the glass, and saw only blackness. The window looked out onto the central patio of the house, and Juan imagined the wide flagstones glistening in the rain. Suddenly he remembered that he had electric light in his house. Perhaps he had forgotten it, having spent his childhood amid red firelight. The walls themselves missed the great trembling silhouettes, growing larger and smaller in time to the foot-

10

steps, as people approached and moved away. Juan looked for the switch and turned it on. The men then appeared brighter and smaller, their eyes squinting in the harshness of the light.

Juan went to put on his coat. While putting his arms in the sleeves, he noticed that his shirt had a big tear, almost over his heart. The shirt was also dirty, with frayed hems and cuffs. A lock of hair fell over his forehead. His head, which was disproportionately large, seemed to wobble over his shoulders. His body, however, was almost stunted, with a sunken chest and twisted legs.

They went out in silence. In the patio, drops of rain stuck like pins in the cracks between the flagstones. Opening the great wooden gate that creaked with dampness, they headed toward the village.

The prison, next to the plaza, was in an old straw loft with one high window. From the center of the plaza came sounds of a childish hubbub mixed with the smell of churned-up mud. The stud pig of the village was usually kept in the jailhouse. At the door, the guards' three-cornered patent leather hats gleamed strangely in the rain. The door opened and Juan Medinao was ushered in.

By the light of a candle he saw the man. He was older than Juan, aged, and his wide-set eyes had a beggar's pleading look. Juan Medinao's heart stopped, as if it had died.

"Hi, Juan Medinao," said the clown. "I'm Dingo, the one who stole your silver coins . . ."

Dingo. Yes, that is who it was, with his eyes spread wide apart like arms on a cross. It was Dingo, betrayer of hopes and dreams. A wave of childhood memories tied Juan's tongue, impeding any word of protest or phrase of welcome. It was Dingo, little Domingo, the game warden's son, the one who had the orange striped cat that looked as if it had been on a grill. Together they had saved and buried coins at the foot of an out-of-the-way and solitary poplar tree, next to the road that led far away. The two of them, in the prime of their youth, when it seemed they could not stand the beatings of their wretched childhood any longer, planned to run away from the village. Juan

Medinao carried in his mind's eye a clear picture of the landscape on that burning morning when he discovered the betrayal. His entire soul trembled; he felt frighteningly childlike. In that land of fire, a shadow was a luxury. And there it was, the shadow of the poplar, straight on the ground, marking forever the flight of his deceitful friend, a thief and lying traveler to nowhere. Together they were going to go to the ocean. Yet on that morning Juan stood alone with his relentless thirst beside the hard shadow of the poplar. That morning he dug through the dirt with feverish hands but found not even a letter, not so much as a mocking letter to dampen his arid desolation. Dingo had left some thirty years ago with a troupe of jugglers and trained dogs. And Juan had stayed behind among dark people who circled grimly over his inheritance with the roving flight of birds of prey. Juan Medinao had remained surrounded by hatred and hunger, heir and master of Lower Artámila, with his crucified God and the enormous head that earned him the mockery of the other children. He had stayed there forever in that exasperated land, amid its dramatic trees and rocks and roads. Seeking heaven in the craggy summits of the mountains, in their gigantic disdain toward life, Juan Medinao had been left by the one person who had neither mocked his big head nor reproached him with handfuls of mud for the hunger of his brothers and sisters. When he was barely twelve years old and everything, from his father to the land, seemed hostile to him, he was also betrayed by Dingo, the one who told lies and invented impossible escapades. It had been so wonderful to listen to Dingo tell about their escape! About running away from the land, the people, the sky, and even from oneself! Dingo, the good-for-nothing, the storyteller, the thief, the merciful one . . .

"I killed the boy, I couldn't avoid it," he was explaining to the thirty-year-old sergeant, with the same expression and the same voice. "And now I'm left without my wagon, without a horse. I don't have a cent to my name. It's the truth. Listen, Juan Medinao, if you

12

still remember me, help me out in the trial and lend me some money so that I can start over again."

Silver coins. Juan Medinao could not remember if they were thirty like the price of Christ, or more than forty, like his age. Silver coins. "Silver coins are no longer in use. Everything seems so long ago!"

Suddenly, Juan Medinao threw himself on Dingo, hugging him, like a leaden cross. It was an attempt at friendly warmth or, perhaps, a desire to crush him with the bitterness of his childhood memories. Thirty years meant nothing. Dingo, surprised by the gesture, remained speechless.

Juan Medinao squeezed him in his arms with the same desolate friendship of his childhood.

"Dingo," he said, "I would have recognized you even if you were dead."

When he left the prison, Juan Medinao looked as if he had been crying. Outside, a servant was waiting with a black umbrella. The deaf-mute was there, leaning against the damp wall, shivering with fear and cold, his hands shoved into his jacket pockets.

"Take this fellow home," Juan Medinao told the servant.

Nobody could drag the dogs away from the jailhouse, and they whined pathetically as they scratched at the door. Poking his head out of the little window as he stood on the straw mattress, Dingo watched the scene below. On his lips he wore a smile that was half-poignant and half-mischievous. The three men moved on up the street. The umbrella with a broken rib looked like an old crow with an injured wing that had landed on their heads.

As soon as Juan Medinao reached the plaza, he stopped.

"Go on home," he told the servant. "Give this fellow something to eat and let him sleep in the stable."

The servant made no reply. He just handed him the umbrella and, followed by the deaf-mute, continued on his way. Juan Medinao remained indecisive. Pedro Cruz was one of his shepherds. He should, as the master, go to the child's wake, thus showing his sympathy. He was not certain which shack was Pedro Cruz's.

In the plaza the children were shrieking, fighting over the brightly colored rags and the shiny gold cords that Dingo had ripped off priests' chasubles long ago when he played the role of devout altar boy. The children's dirty little fists defended ribbons or remnants. Farther on, the loose wheel lay on the ground, miraculously still spinning. One child fell on the ground, dragging a long yellow tail. The childrens' little bare feet made no noise on the smashed boards of the wagon. The trunk, with its broken laughing lid, revealed its weightless treasures. So many smiles painted on cardboard! There was only one mask that cried: a white mask, with moon-green drooping features and a blue mouth. A towheaded girl held it against her face and poked her head out of the wagon window. Although it was already night and growing dark, Juan Medinao took everything in: the colors, the rapid footsteps, and the greedy little hands. The children dragged the costumes through the mud. They knew nothing of the carnival for which Juan Medinao prayed and beat his chest in his room. The carnival that made him protect those who made fun of his big head and the one who stole his childhood savings; that which led him to the wake of the shepherd's son. They knew nothing of carnival as he did. The rain continued to beat down without mercy on the colors; without pity for that long green feather, that beautiful green feather that was now being trailed through the muck. The rain had spoiled Dingo's party and had left everything drenched and useless. All the masks had tears running down their noses. Perhaps they were taking revenge for the silver coins.

Juan Medinao advanced toward the wrecked wagon. At his approach the children scattered like a flock of wild birds. He grabbed the wrist of the small towheaded girl, who pressed the mask harder against her face in a stubborn desire for refuge.

14

"Tell me, where does Pedro Cruz live?" he demanded. The girl's wrist was as slippery as a snake. Figuring that she did not understand, he rephrased the question: "Tell me where the dead child lives."

The girl led him. She went ahead of him, tiny, splashing through the puddles with her quick bare feet. They arrived at a hut made of stone and red dirt. A poster promoting wolf hunting hung on the wall. It was tattered and moldy from dampness. Juan Medinao remembered somewhat vaguely the recent ravages of his flocks. Last winter Pedro Cruz had fled from the wolves. Perhaps even now, at this very moment, he was being stalked by them. There was only one large low window and a door in the hut. Within he saw flames glowing in the fireplace. He could hear the women moaning inside. Juan Medinao and the girl peered through the window. The windowpanes seemed to cry. He saw a little board that hung from two ropes, swinging back and forth. The girl pointed it out to him and said something incomprehensible.

Juan Medinao pushed open the door. In the kitchen, next to the fire, the child was laid out on a stretcher. He lay there all white, the blood washed off and his hair freshly combed. His mother and neighbor women were gathered together wailing. As he entered they suddenly grew silent. Only the swing kept on swaying as if pushed by invisible and cruel childish hands.

Once more, his anger choked him. There they were again, those eyes like the heads of black pins staring at him, sullen and spiteful. The master had come in. Nothing could protect him from those eyes, neither his humiliation nor his prayers as he knelt on the ground. This gesture of attending the wake meant nothing to them. Were they going to blame him for the death of the child as well? He began to play nervously with a button on his vest. His anger flared; it went to his head and drowned him in its turbulent red wine. The shepherd's hut smelled of poverty and dirt. All at once, it was as if everything accused him, Juan Medinao, the master. Surely at night the rats chewed the ropes of the swing and the soles of their canvas shoes. Those wet shoes left to dry near the fire that now were exuding a sickening steam.

"Let us pray," he told them. And his voice held all of the sharp dryness of an order. No one seemed to have heard him.

"Pray, women," he repeated, interlacing his own soft, warm fingers. Someone had without a bit of irony placed a flower in the dead child's mouth. It must have been a paper flower, because that month the countryside had been parched. And so the child lay with the wire stem between his lips, oblivious to the fact that he had been spared forever from thirst. His mother sobbed in anguish.

"Are you going to stay?" asked one of the women. There was neither fear nor affection in her voice. Not even courtesy. The women of this land could speak as if time spoke, beyond indifference. Suddenly it seemed that the women lacked eyes and mouths; he saw only the withering bulks of their bodies and their coarse, matted hair. Kneeling on the floor, he fumbled in his pockets for his rosary. Through the window he saw the face of the towheaded girl putting on her mask and taking it off again. She put it on and took it off. On the other side of the swing, the rain and the red brilliance of the fire.

The mother stood up and walked away from her child. Still weeping, she began to grind a small handful of coffee that she had kept in a can since the last funeral.

16

3

Abruptly Juan Medinao bowed his head and began to pray. His prayer had nothing to do with his voice. His prayer was a return to adolescence, to childhood. To solitude.

The towheaded girl had disappeared from the window. She had returned into the night again, leaving the mask forgotten on the windowsill. The painted face, with down-turned features, cried hypocritically in the rain. It was carnival. (And so it was always: all men and all women who approached his closed windows returned to the deep night from whence they had come. They might leave him a mask leaning against the window pane. The black night surrounding their acts and thoughts. And he, blind in the night.)

He had been born during carnival, forty-two years ago, on a restless afternoon. The wind whipped around the corners, making clothes stick to the body and hair to the forehead. The trees of the Northwest Cemetery bent over, shaking, and in the patio a dog was barking. His mother, that woman with the thin black waist who used to fling herself face down on the bed to whine and moan, had told him about it. When he was barely three, his mother recounted the events of that afternoon during carnival in which she cast him into the world. Holding his head between her bony and feverish hands, she said: "It was nearly nightfall; I could see the sky from my bed. I saw it turn green, just like a man when he is about to vomit. I thought

17

I was going to die, that I wouldn't be able to stand it. Juan Senior was absent, and the doctor arrived drunk, as usual, slumped over his horse and splattered with mud. Your father had brought me here from far away, from my town where there were stores and a church. Here I felt buried alive and as lonely as the dead."

In the village, they said that his mother was mad, crazy, possessed by the devil, in the red house where shadows always lurked in the corners. Shadows that he now tried to obliterate with electric light in order to expose childhood memories. He had spent his early years terrified of black corners, of steps that creaked in the dark, and of bats that stuck to his cold bedroom walls. His first memories of his father were dreadful. Juan Senior was brutality, fear, an overwhelming, remote force. His slaps on the back burned like humiliation. Above all, he was laughter: a foreign language to young Juan's sensibility, to his hesitant living as an ugly child. Cruel and impossible laughter that he could never manage.

He remembered his father one day standing in the center of the patio. His legs, like tree trunks, were stuffed into leather boots that reached to his knees. He looked as if he had sprouted from the ground, vibrant son of the earth, with a cascade of black curls from his beard trembling on his chest. He shook his head when he laughed. The sound from his throat was always laughter, even when he swore or threatened. And there in the middle of the patio with his whip in hand, he watched as they skinned a bull that had died in the ravine. All of a sudden he raised the whip in his hand and lashed the carcass. Two maids who stood nearby laughed boisterously. Juan Junior, who didn't know how to play, saw the white line of the whiplash turn redder and redder and melt into a red-hot foam that fell onto the ground in drops like fire. The drops were flowers. Flowers of an impossible force and with a pungent aroma that caused his skin to twitch. Little Juan, his head too large for his body, covered his ears with his hands and fled from the patio, where his father stayed reveling in the maids' laughter.

Juan Junior was just four years old, with nowhere to turn.

One day the parish priest from Central Artámila came to pay them a visit and to eat cookies with half a walnut in the center. Juan and his mother listened respectfully to what the priest had to say. His mother held her head down, her long eyelashes fluttering on her cheeks, and twisted a corner of her shawl between her fingers. The priest patted Juan's shoulders and told him that one day, all dressed in white, he could swallow God. "And ask him for favors," timidly added his mother. Then Juan Junior learned that for the rest of his life he should pray for the salvation of his father. For him and for all strong and thoughtless sinners who beat raw flesh with a whip. And also for pale and eternally offended women who cry facedown on the bed. And for old parish priests who suffer from asthma and must walk eight kilometers eating red dust in order to carry the word of God to forgetful and hardened people.

Early on he understood that Juan Senior was playful and generous, cruel and godless. His powerful voice made the silver medallion on Juan Junior's chest tremble. His father's eyes were bright: hunter's eyes, shining, often angry, yet cheerful. Eyes of frost and wine, of poisonous flowers. Those flowers that grew next to the river, among the gypsy canes, and that when cut stained your fingers with a juice that should never touch your lips. All of the stinginess and greed of Grandfather Juan were transformed into the carefree spending of his son. He was a spendthrift, a braggart, and a drunk. He had not wanted to marry a peasant, and for that reason, one day he brought home a well-manicured woman, tearful and frightened, from a town far beyond the mountains, where there were shop windows filled with colorful ribbons, rosaries made of gold, and bottles of cologne. And he did not even love this woman. Often he would abandon her in the big house and go off beyond the last Artámila. He would forget them and the land. Later he would return with objects from distant cities, which gathered mold piled up in his room. He began drinking more and more. A garnet-red wine and another

19

wine as golden as the harvest moon. He would become like the cold wind that slams the doors shut and scares the leaves in October. Then he would go away. He always went away. Juan Junior would watch him ride his horse across the patio, pass through the stockade fence, and shut the great wooden gate behind him. His father would always delay his return. He would go away like all men and women, like the sweet mauve tones of winter, like the grape harvest and the leaves. And when his father came home, young Juan would cry about what he had smiled at before, and he would smile at what used to make him cry. But he, Juan Junior, was always the same. Always so alone: with his mother's moody silence and the teasing of the laborers' children, who would laugh at his oversized head and his twisted legs.

In the dining room of the big house, where there hung a dried-up and yellowed portrait of Grandfather Juan, he would look at himself in the mirror, amazed that he came from this land that sheltered rats, flowers like suns, and blue snakes. All of it was to be his one day. The laborers' work, and that of their sons, would belong to him. Almost all of Lower Artámila, from the run-down vineyard on the slope whose late fruit was killed by the winter to the high golden fields of summer. "Oh somber land, dark land, that gives and takes like God!" He was so different from all that surrounded him!

His mother reminded him of the dark corner of the drawing room, which was gloomy and never cleaned by the maids: the epitome of blackness, ghost stories, superstitions, and candles to San Antonio. The black beads of her rosary, like a caravan of ants on a business trip to her soul, looped over her wrist where her blood pulsed erratically.

Outside in the patio, under a sky bluer and more remarkable than ever, the field hands and servants were celebrating the August festival of the wheat harvest. The flagstones in the central patio had, like butterfly wings, a perennial golden dust on them. Bright straw gleamed in the cracks between the flagstones. One of the servants

20

knew how to play the fiddle. Accompanied by the guitar, he produced strange, whining songs. The music was languid, with a shifting rhythm and a thick sweetness that got into your veins and made you toss and turn in bed. That night, Juan Junior could not bear it any longer. The warm, sticky rhythm ruffled the white curtains in his bedroom. He crept downstairs barefoot and hid behind one of the columns of the great central patio. There he saw them dancing and drinking. They were laughing in low and sinister tones, like the water that hollows out the core of the countryside.

It was then that he noticed the sudden splendor of the maid Salome. Until that moment, she was just another girl with sunburnt skin and a white blouse. But now someone had given her silver earrings and an extraordinary new dress. The dress, indeed her whole person, was almost outrageous amid the dull uniformity of the women of Artámila. The dress was green with pink stripes. Unexpectedly she appeared like a great exotic insect, celebrating the harvest in the center of the music, on the golden dust of the flagstones. Her shadow, under the rapid turns of her bare chestnut-colored feet, was a blue elastic stain that enticed him to stretch out his hands and submerge them in it as if in a very cold pool of water. His pale childish hands, with their chewed fingernails and burning wrists. Without being told, he, Juan Junior, at four years of age, had discovered the truth. He had figured it out without knowing anything, without ever having seen them together. And, all around Salome, the three heavy wings of the house, the high mountains, the rain, the black moths, the crows cawing, and the winds howling in the Northwest Cemetery could do nothing to dull the green and pink of her dress or to silence the music of her silver earrings.

From that night on, Juan Senior and Salome both terrified and attracted him; they made him want to flee and take refuge in God or in the Northwest Cemetery. His mother told him that Salome was a bad woman, but he could not put her out of his mind because his father was alive, rooted in the land, violent and lively like a relentless bonfire. Nobody could throw her out into the street. Her very existence was fascinating, even when the dress became tattered and was used to frighten away birds in the springtime, even when she went back to wearing the coarse white blouse and he saw her eating with her fingers in the field. She laughed as she lay on the straw and raised her arms toward the sun, revealing large sweat stains in her armpits. Juan Senior and Salome were like a flooded river or like the fiery red dirt that the wind threw against little Juan's closed window.

Meanwhile, his mother was an exasperated little witch, with livid eyes and lips white with pride. Oh, when Juan Junior was born, there was a reason the dogs barked in the patio with the moths. "That evil woman," his mother would tell him, holding back her tears, "will burn in the black fire of hell." It seemed to him that he was still listening to his mother's unseemly laughter as she raved about what would happen to Salome in the afterlife.

Then young Juan's heart would sink into God: into that God who had bells in Central Artámila. And he loved Him and trusted Him, because he could not love or expect anything from the burning fields, or from the cracking whips, or from the men and women who got lost in the furrows and became smaller and smaller toward the horizon. Although he knew not the whys and wherefores of God, he had faith in Him. His faith was like the salt from the sea, which he did not know either. He had not yet begun to read the catechism, and the day he took it in his hands for the first time, he felt afraid. "They are going to spoil it for me," he knew by intuition. It was to oblige him to think of God, and God should have been left as He was: in his heart, pure and primary. He was five years old, only five years old, and nevertheless, he knew all this. He knew it as he knew that in the autumn all living things would perish. As he knew that the beautiful grapevine that his father had planted would not be made into wine for harsh and frugal Artámila, where bread and water sufficed under the storm and fire of summer. He learned everything so early, and from the time he was a small child, he held in his heart the yeast of existence, which fermented in him and sickened him for his entire life.

One day, although he was still very small, his mother sent him away to school with the recommendation that he be taught only to pray. The school, with brown walls and a leaky roof from which dead nests hung, was far away on the road that led to distant lands. It had no garden. The windows were slashed, and when it rained everything creaked, the wooden benches and the pictures of the Gospel. A little book fell into his hands. It was small, tiny, next to the tomes of arithmetic and geography. It had engravings and said on the first page: "YOU WILL MAKE THE SIGN OF THE CROSS." The teacher explained it to him while scratching one ear with a toothpick, because Juan did not know how to read yet. It was necessary to move his ink-stained thumb from his forehead to his lips. No, no, not like that! God was greater and more serious. Perhaps only the bells could have prayed to Him. The teacher was bald, and he read the catechism wearily, amid tobacco smoke. With nicotine-stained teeth, he would speak of the love of God. Juan did not want to return to that school; he did not want to see the teacher or the other children ever again.

Around that time, something transcendental happened in his life. Pablo, son of Salome, was born. It was in August, a violent and burnt season, when the greenery had died away and the wet holes in the road had turned to black dust.

Salome herself seemed to disappear. It was as if only the tinkling of her earrings remained around her nonexistent face. As if the imaginary music of her earrings sang of a woman who had never been born. Salome's steps resembled a duck's, and her swollen belly destroyed the grace of her fifteen years. His father went away again.

One morning, Juan Junior woke to the sound of footsteps in the patio. Next to the stable slept an old maidservant who helped to bring calves and men into the world. Sitting up in bed, he listened with a longing heart. In his bones he felt a premonition of his brother's arrival. Excitedly he jumped out of bed, put on his shirt and pants, and ran barefoot down to the patio.

Outside, the mosquitoes hummed and sparkled, forming an integral part of the heat. He saw the hurrying figure of the old woman, swearing at the interruption of her sleep. Buttoning up the last of her innumerable skirts, she ran behind Salome's older sister. Everything else remained quiet and indifferent under the rose-colored moon. The other servants slept, exhausted from the day's work. The great gate of the fence creaked open. The two women ran toward the laborers' huts. A honey-colored light shone on the ground, where the fence posts projected long shadow arms toward him. Conquering his fear, he followed them to where Salome lived with her sister and young Agustín.

The women entered and shut the door. Panting from his run, young Juan sat down on the ground leaning his back against the hut wall.

Then all grew quiet. He heard only the vibrant silence of the blood in his temples and the noise of the insects, haunting and bluish, in the darkness that came over him. All of a sudden Rosa, Salome's older sister, began to shout, waking up Agustín and ordering him to go outside. The cat slipped through the yellow crack in the door and fled out to the field. In the corner of the hut, a water pipe emptied into a wooden bucket. It was the one hut with a small water tank, Agustín's invention, whose strange mechanism nobody had yet managed to figure out. It began to drip. Each little drop of water, rhythmically spaced and musical, was like a luminous ticking away of passing seconds, sparkling under the moonlight. Suddenly the door opened and Agustín, still grimy from his father's fields, came out. The moon's radiance haloed his head. Little Juan pressed close to the wall and held his breath. Agustín hesitated a second. He was half-naked and carried two buckets. His skinny rigid arms hung down along his sides. Then he disappeared behind the other huts,

24

going in the direction of the river, for his small tank of water had been used up.

Juan slipped in through the door that Agustín had left open. To the right was a dark space where they kept farming tools and a leather whip that made him flinch. Juan crouched down amid the rakes and the scythes. He sensed, without hearing it, a long cry. And he saw the vapor of the water boiling in the kitchen. A man was being born, right there, behind the door to the bedroom. Maybe he would look like Juan himself. . . ? No. No. Nobody would ever be like him. He was alone among the rest. Why had he been born? His tears, long and slow, fell warm onto his hand. His five years seemed shaken by the awareness of his solitude. Perhaps he was cursed. But his God would save him from mankind. He still had to wait, who knows for how long! And if he were to die? The thought occurred to him that as his brother was being born he might die. Yes. They would find him the following day amid the hoes and the pickaxes, like a dilapidated doll. But he did not die. And that long wait was just the beginning of the one he would endure even until today.

For a moment, Juan thought: "If this child is born, maybe I won't be alone anymore." But a son of Juan Senior and Salome would be like a river crossing over dried-out plains under a great sun. On a small board, a thin candle kept its flame. Two flies chased each other around it, and he heard the melted wax fall on the wooden floor. He loved fire and always carried matches in his pocket in order to light twigs and straw in the corner of the patio, when everybody was in the fields and nobody, except the dogs or his mother, could see. A violent desire then assailed him: to set the hut afire and to die next to his as yet unborn brother. To die, the two of them, so that the wind might sweep them away together and fling them toward the uncertain horizon. But almost immediately he realized that it was a crime that would stain the whiteness of his soul. Only then did he try to see how men are born. They had forced Agustín to jump up from his sleep

25

and go out to the fields. Maybe they had sent him away because it was ugly. Speaking of the afternoon when young Juan was born, his mother had described it as "horrible." Now, neither the wind nor the dogs were howling. A hot and oppressive silence drenched the hair and foreheads of those awaiting the birth. The candle went out, and the remaining wick turned blue, like a little worm that was dying.

Suddenly the bedroom door seemed to come alive – like an imposing black force in front of him. It was an old wooden door, whose ill-fitting boards let yellow slashes of light escape. Slowly he approached and, pressing his face to the door, peered through one of the cracks. At first he saw nothing; then he observed only a piece of wall stained with dampness. The smell of woodworm and mold overcame him. His sweaty forehead stuck to the wood. In this position, he saw a black spider clumsily climbing up to the ceiling. He remained still until it disappeared from his narrow visual field. He heard footsteps and voices. But nobody wailed; nobody moaned. Then he clearly understood that Salome would never again be the queen of the harvest festival. Her green-and-pink dress was now just faded tatters. Oh, he did not want to see, he did not need to see anything! His heart beat madly. He turned and ran out.

At the threshold, he tripped on a step and fell to the ground. Face downward, he felt the searing heat of the earth in all its cruelty. Painfully he sat up and looked at his knees, which began to ooze dark blood. A long nearly black drop of blood snaked its way down his leg. At that moment, she left the bedroom and saw him. It was Rosa. She approached him with her wet hands on her hips. He raised his head and their eyes met, quietly. Little Juan was not crying anymore. But his neck seemed to be trembling slightly with a childish hiccough. Rosa was some thirty years old. Around her eyelids were crumpled fine slashes of time. A thin braid fell on her shoulders. She was half-dressed, her skin divided between two colors: paler where the sun never reached. All was withered in her. Her body, whose fruits had been harvested early, was already old and exhausted. Although she

26

felt no pity for the boy, as she felt none for Salome or for the child being born, she bent down, took the master's child by the arm, and brought him into the kitchen. All her life she had worked for those who did not matter to her, for things that did not even belong to her.

The fire in the kitchen had been recently lit, and the logs were still fresh. Steam covered the windowpanes and made one's breath burn. Without talking, she washed his knees. Then she opened the door to the street and shut it behind him.

Outside, Juan dried his tears with his forearm. From behind the mountains another fiery day was bursting forth. Overwhelmed by an uncertain power, he set forth toward the first hill where the threshing floors were located. He just could not go home and sleep. His brother had been born. On the first threshing floor, the half-cleaned wheat was piled up. The heat weighed heavily in an oppressive silence. The flagstones of the threshing floor were still hot, and he lay face down, his head buried in his arms. He was only five years old, but a thousand precocious sorrows made him lie down and suffer in the face of life. He had heard much silence and many words. He was one of those who goes around on tiptoe, pressing his ear to keyholes. Juan Junior let himself go completely on the ground, and slowly, sensually, his love and his hatred for his brother were born. "He may be beautiful and strong," whispered an angel in his ear. He looked at his pale hands, grimy with dirt. A wave of blood came over him, an intense flush of blood that sickened him, and reddened his brain and the inside of his eyelids. Then, without even knowing how, he fell asleep.

The boisterous shouting of the peasants arriving at the threshing floor with their horses woke him up. Juan set off running again. He did not want to be seen. He could not bear the thought that they might see him and think: "How beautiful and strong his brother is!" Childishly, he believed that his brother was already a man, and not a weak, reddish baby like any newborn.

A voice from down below had been calling him for some time. It was a servant from the house looking for him. Most certainly, his mother was worried about him. He ran up river toward the mountain. He stopped for a moment and looked back, panting from his run, and watched the threshing floor in a senseless terror of everything. Sunlight fell on a girl who was sitting on a footstool beneath a great pile of hay. Since she was only three or four years old, she had not begun working yet. Across her lap she held the rigid body of a doll. A toy: something extraordinary, even unheard of, among the village children! The doll had long yellow hair hanging down to the ground, which the girl caressed with thin, delicate fingers. Juan started running again, this time even faster. Everything hurt him so! As he followed the bank of the river, running between the willows, he discovered tracks left by a greyhound and finally came across a shepherd watching his flock. The man was not a servant of Juan's family; he kept his own sheep. An old man, he was sitting on a stone with his hands on his knees. His hair had not been cut in a long time, and it fell in white tufts on his neck. Silent and indifferent, his eyes stared into emptiness. Young Juan approached him, urged on by the same feeling that earlier had made him lie down on the stones of the threshing floor. He sat down at the old man's feet. How much he needed peace! He was very small, and the shadow of the old shepherd's years plunged him into a sweet sleep, like a lullaby. He did not want to know so many things, to feel so many things. His bones were still like green reeds; his hands, barely formed yet. The shepherd's smell of leather reached him, as did the odors of the awakening countryside, with blades of grass sprouting up happily like children. The old man, on the other hand, seemed to be made of stone, less human than the oak trees and the clouds.

Juan raised his head and said in a high-pitched voice: "Someone was born."

The shepherd remained impassive. Juan then added, "In the Zácaros' hut, to Salome."

The shepherd only replied: "Whore."

Little Juan went back to sleep. When he woke again, pebbles from the ground were embedded in his cheeks. The shepherd, who was sitting farther uphill, was cutting off hunks of bread. He cut off one piece for the dog and another for himself. Juan approached him and ate as well. All of a sudden, the old man pressed the point of the knife onto the child's chest. As if he had been thinking about his words until that moment, he burst out violently, "Look at him," as if he were addressing the greyhound. "What is this one going to do with Artámila? I saw how his grandfather, the old goat, took it over. I owe them nothing, but woe to the others! Since then, who in the village is not in debt to the Juans? I remember the year of the influenza outbreak, when my children were dying. That old man came to my house with his deceitful promise of loans. But I threw stones at him and told him: 'Get out, you old miser, you won't drink my blood, even if we all burn up under the sun.' He only had one son, and a stupid and evil one at that! And from him came this stunted child with a big head. Oh yes, they're doing well, that family of thieves! Who knows, little one, if you don't rot in the ground with the dirt between your teeth beforehand, this newborn child just might make some trouble for you!"

He spat and put the loaf of bread back in his pouch. For the rest of the day Juan followed the old man around silently.

Toward evening he returned with him to the village, long shadows galloping behind them. Juan passed by the laborers' huts. Nighttime was blotting out everything, dimming the colors, and leaving only white skeletal forms under the moonlight. The little girl's footstool beside the pile of hay was now empty. Mosquitoes, in sparkling clouds, continued their humming in the oppressive heat.

Juan could barely feel his body. The day's fasting had made him faint. His little person flickered like a wavering flame. Slowly he walked toward his house, in a straight line, as if hallucinating. The entire sky was dying of thirst.

If his father had returned, he would beat him naked. And if not, his mother would hold his head between her hands, complaining of his absence. She would tell him that a good boy should not run away from home.

In the village, something unusual was happening. The gate of the stockade fence had been left open. The moon had paused over the rooftops. In the patio, three women were sitting in a row on the ground, their shawls over their heads, their hands dropped in their laps. Peasants' hands, lying idly on their black skirts. Seeing this, Juan knew that something out of the ordinary had happened. His feet stopped. Then he realized that the women were looking at him, along with the stable boy, and the moon. Oh, quiet moon! Nobody had ever told Juan the story of the old man who carried firewood to the moon, but the moonlight had caught his eyes as well, as it captures the attention of all children. At the door of the house, one of the maids appeared. On seeing him, she covered her face as if she were going to cry. Juan understood that he should keep advancing, approaching the house until a superior force detained him. He crossed the patio and climbed the steps. In his mother's room there was light, and on the floor was outlined the yellow square of the door. It was a special light with its own smell, taste, and touch. There was nothing violent or dazzling about it. Delicately, it wiped out the darkness like a breath. He continued on, tiny and solemn, with his arms hanging by his sides. On crossing the threshold, his shadow barely left a black flickering on the floor. There was a stellar trembling all throughout him, like a quivering blade of grass.

He stood at last by the foot of the bed. Rigid, with her face covered, death was laid out on the bed. There, with her thin black waist and yellow hands that would no longer hold his head. The room seemed to be full of buzzing flies. Then all the heat of the evening rolled away at once. Through his fingernails and eyes winter came in, and he felt as if his blood were flowing out of him like a river. He was a child and only five years old! In the next moment, he was hugging her frantically, without a single heartbeat. It was as if life had stopped for him and now he could never go back to breathing. He ripped the handkerchief off, and he saw her face all swollen, purplish, and tinged with blood. She had hanged herself.

When the animal sound of his own voice surprised him, the servants came in and dragged him away from the dead woman. Then, like a flock of birds, they disappeared around corners and behind closed doors. But nothing would ever erase that vision of her open eyes. Henceforth, whenever he remembered that night, he saw, instead of his mother's face, a pair of eyes with red and blue veins, like ribbons on a bull's back floating in the wind. He howled for her like a dog, stretched out on the straw mat on the floor, pierced by solitude, outraged, with his green and bitter child's love broken. Dead mother. Dead mother. These two words wounded him with a blade of ice. How pale the moon had grown! They could not take him out of the room. He clung to the floor ferociously. His throat filled with fire, hoarse with sobbing. As dawn broke, amid the murmuring of the servants' prayers, he fell asleep.

The racket of the horse's hooves startled him. They had sent word to Juan Senior. The light of the entering sun made the room red and gold, and the linen curtains seemed to burn. His shoulders still shook with a quiet, deep desperation that he could not even comprehend. He was grief-stricken. His nose was runny, and his face was streaked with tears. In the window, a bee was trying to get in through a fold in the curtain.

The horse's hooves clattered on the flagstones of the patio. Then the well-known and dreaded footsteps approached, making the stairs creak.

Slowly, young Juan got up. He looked like a little waxen saint. His father came in. He had never seemed so large and ruddy. With him a strong odor entered the room, as if the entire forest had begun to blow through the cracks. The smell of resin and new leather dis-

31

placed the fog of buzzing and death. Juan Senior stood still watching him, his eyes filled with terror.

Abruptly the man seemed to give in. Shaken with pain and fear, he looked closely at little Juan. He took his son in his arms and sat him on his lap. Juan Senior was crying without tears, and in that weeping there was something like a painful surprise, the surprise of a huge bestial child that released him from guilt. And then, through the man's dry weeping, young Juan miraculously had a sense of his father for the first time. He guessed that there was no real evil in him. He was just stupid. His crying was very much like his laughter. It was his same old laughter.

Something collapsed in front of Juan Junior. His father had lost distance, had lost strength. He was just another sinner, one of those sinners for whom he had been taught to pray. An ordinary sinner, like one who does not go to mass or one who steals fruit. Little Juan sat stiffly on his father's knees. Near his cheeks, the man's rough lips produced a deep, earthy, howling noise that was almost palpable. Juan Junior began to feel white, cold, and far off like an angel.

At that moment, his father took the boy's hands and kissed them awkwardly.

"It's all my fault, all my fault. I am to blame. She was as crazy as a loon, damn it! What the hell. . . , she was your mother, and now because of me, all because of me, you're left without her! How was it that I didn't realize that she was mad enough to do something like this? My poor son, forgive me!"

The bee was now still and silent, caught in the curtain like a gold button. Juan Junior's feeling of weakness left him. He had become the strong one. His strength was thick and could drown a person, slowly and sweetly, like an evil honey. His father's final words took shape: forgive me. Forgive me. Even his suffering stopped, but he understood it. A burning wine entered his veins and flooded his brain. Young Juan reached up his hand, and without any timidity, he caressed his father's head. He did not love him. He would never love him. But he had just discovered a sword he would always carry in his right hand. A sword he would never leave behind. It was forgiveness against his fellow man, the leaden forgiveness of the weak.

In the meantime, the brutal man kept repeating, "My poor son. . . !"

But that was almost forty years ago.

4

"You don't know how much you hurt me . . . But I forgive you. I forgave you the very next day, as soon as I saw that you had run off with the money," he told his old friend, the only friend he had ever had in his life.

Meanwhile, Dingo's eyes were saying: "But, come on now, those were just foolish things from our childhood!" Nevertheless, he stole furtive glances at the ground and at his manacled hands. First they were going to take him to Central Artámila where the judge lived. Then in Nájera they would put him on trial. Juan Medinao had come to offer his support. As always.

"Dingo, I know what you're thinking: that it was only the small-time thieving of children without any real consequences. Well, maybe you're right. But listen to me: you stole my freedom and spoiled my life. Yes, you spoiled it and left me without a single friend . . ."

What passion there was in his voice as he continued: "Or don't you remember those days?"

The policemen were ready. With the heels of their boots, they stomped out the embers of the fire they had built to warm themselves before setting out on the road. Their ugly mood and swearwords filled the air. Dingo's hands were turning blue from the handcuffs and the cold. "Now he's going to start preaching, but I've got to be patient. In the end, he'll help me and maybe he'll even buy me a new wagon . . . And when that happens, he won't see hide or hair of me! And I'll never have to see him or this God-forsaken land ever again!" He had always been like that, ever since they were children. Juan Medinao always had to tell pious stories before he lent a dime. But he would lend it, and not demand it back. "Everybody puts on his own little show, each one in his own way," Dingo told himself philosophically.

The sky had cleared and was turning pink behind the black skeletons of the trees. Juan Medinao stood before him, his feet in the mud, trembling with cold as he spoke and holding together the lapels of his jacket with one hand. A sharp wind blew his graying hair about. His rheumy eyes were still the same as when he was a boy, as if he had a cold. Nor had his voice changed: a harsh, low voice, which sometimes broke in a passionate and incomprehensible trembling. The sinister tone of his voice often did not harmonize with his words.

"Don't you remember anymore?" Juan repeated. He was insistent, like a drunk. Dingo nodded his head.

He thought: "The least he could do is give me a drink."

As if he had guessed his thoughts, one of the policemen offered Dingo the wineskin and helped him to drink by holding it over his lips.

"Move on," they told him. They wrapped themselves up in their capes and got into the wagon, the only one in the village, lent to them by Juan Medinao so they would not have to walk.

"Good-bye, my friend," said Dingo in the pathetic tone he used in his best theatrical moments. "Thanks for your help."

"Of course you can count on me," Juan said. "You're my friend, my best friend, who . . ."

The screeching of the wheels and the carter's shout drowned out his words. He began to walk quickly behind the wagon and screamed with his hands cupped around his mouth like a megaphone: "Dingo, don't worry, don't worry! I'll go to Nájera. I'll stand by you in every-thing. . . ! I'll take care of your bail, you'll come home, and then. . . !"

Sticking out of the wagon like a marionette, Dingo went away, with his pleading smile, his beard blowing in the wind, and his wide-set eyes in mischievous triumph. Violent anger boiled in Juan Medi-nao's chest. "Count on me, friend!" he repeated. And he stopped to watch him go off in the distance.

The doctor and the priest were arriving now, passing Dingo on the road. Their horses were splattered with mud. Juan stopped to take a look at the priest. The old parish priest of the Artámilas had died not long ago; this was the new one in the parish, still unknown to Juan. He was very young, pale, and wore wire-rimmed glasses. He had not been long out of the seminary. As he watched him, Juan ex-perienced a feeling similar to that which came over him before he ate a baby partridge. A perverse delight comforted him.

Juan approached them and shook the hand of the old drunk who helped deliver him into the world. The doctor was now a wreck of a man, with purplish lips hanging down. His medical bag had become softened in the rain.

The priest did not wait for Juan to hold his horse but jumped down to the ground. The hem of his cassock was wet and muddy. He had, besides, great drops of wax on his chest and sleeves. With a timid gesture, he pushed the bridge of his glasses up his nose, his lips trembling slightly. Juan approached him and softly touched his sleeve.

"Father," he said, "will you hear my confession? I can take com-munion only once or twice a year. Here, Father, you see how we live. We have to travel eight kilometers to go to mass and take commu-nion at the parish church. And, of course, I am no longer young or in very good health."

36

5

They entered the house of the Juans. The doctor sat down next to the fire with a bottle in his hand. The dogs surrounded him and began to bark at him affectionately. On the table a heavy and plentiful meal had been served. After one look, the priest blushed, certain that he would not be able to take a bite.

When the dinner was over, Juan led the priest to a side room where a wooden cross hung on the wall. The priest sat down on a chair, looking toward the window, with the stole around his neck and his hands crossed. Juan Medinao knelt down at his feet and, with no preamble, without even crossing himself, said in his harshest voice: "I am an arrogant man. Pride poisons me, and although I try to fight it and humble my heart, many times in my life it has gotten the best of me!"

Many times, that was certain. When he was ten years old, he became aware of it for the first time.

After his mother's funeral, his father had taken him far away from Artámila to shut him up in a private school. Juan Junior's presence at home gave him a guilty conscience. Juan Senior's first outbursts of repentance gradually turned into bitter disgust every time he crossed glances with his tiny son. Juan Senior was too healthy for feelings of repentance to torture him for long. His son's presence soon became as disagreeable as the scent of lavender, which reminded him of his dead wife's clothes. One morning he took the child to a boarding school. They rode to a beautiful town, and from there a green carriage took them to the largest town that young Juan could even imagine. Accustomed to his mountains, the little boy tripped on the edges of the sidewalks as he looked up at the buildings and into the shop windows.

The school was on the outskirts of the town, in the rolling countryside. But those hills were gentle, so different from the rocks and woods of Artámila. As he said good-bye to his father, Juan Junior, his little suitcase in hand, felt overwhelmed by an unknown melancholy.

Five years went by. During that time he made no friends, just as in the village. He was different from everybody there as well, and he had to pardon the same mockery that he had forgiven the peasant children of Artámila. Awkward and unattractive, he won neither the affection of the teachers nor that of the boys. During recess, he sat alone on a bench, and without bitterness or happiness, he watched the others play. In truth, he knew he was different, distant from others; not even their jokes about his head managed to affect him. He was a special creature, who prayed to God to take him away from mankind soon. Already then he was arrogant but did not know it. Sometimes in church, he felt himself bathed in unexpected tears, without knowing exactly why. The religion teacher did not manage to get him to learn the catechism and would punish him for impiety by making him kneel for a long time.

During summer vacations, he returned to Artámila, where he stayed confined to the house, playing in the granary with boxes of matches, rosaries, pictures, and glass beads. He set up a little altar, with pieces of cloth, and buried dead birds. He stayed as far apart from the laborers' children and his father as he did from his teachers and classmates. In those five years, he never saw his brother. Sometimes, however, Juan remembered him, but he put him out of his mind uneasily, preferring to ignore his existence. "Maybe he's dead," he often thought with an odd sense of relief. On one occasion, his father brought him a cardboard horse. One of its ears broke off, and the black hole where the ear had been produced a weird sense of terror in him. He hid the horse in the granary and never played with it again. He wanted to be a saint, in the same way other boys want to be aviators or bullfighters.

One summer vacation, when he was ten years old, he found his father at home, half-crippled. He had fallen from a horse. With his leg in a splint stretched over a bench and his arm in a sling, he was in a very bad mood. To help pass the time more pleasurably, he kept a pitcher of wine by his side and deafened the household by shouting insults and swearwords. Since he was bored, he showed a sudden interest in Juan Junior's progress at school, and he soon realized that his son, at ten, barely knew how to read or add numbers. He swore, threatened him with his fist, and finally said: "You'll always be a sullen peasant! Don't ask me what that big head's going to do for you, or what might be inside of it! Well, it's best that you leave that expensive, no-good school. Since in the long run you are going to end up with all of this, you're old enough to stay here and begin to get to know it. Even though you're just a skinny little runt."

Juan Senior remained thoughtful for a moment and finally said, as if it were impossible for him to hold back the words that he most wanted to keep silent: "If only you had seen Pablo Zácaro the other day! What a devil of a child! He's more mischievous and clever than seven old wise men put together! And he's only five years old. . . , I think. Juan, son, aren't you ashamed to know that a baby half your age knows how to read and rattle off his numbers, even when he hasn't been able to go to school and most likely will never be able to go?"

Something cold overwhelmed young Juan's heart. Pablo Zácaro could not be anyone but Salome's son. In his father's words there was an irrepressible pride, hiding like a thief. Although he had never recognized Salome's son as his own, everybody knew that the Zácaro boy was his.

39

That night, Juan Junior could not sleep. A new and overpowering sorrow consumed him. "So he hasn't died. He's alive. He's alive right now, at this very moment, he's living like me." The brother. Another person with his blood, with his same blood, living beneath the same sky. Another who was perhaps one of God's chosen. He bit his fist. A strange uneasiness kept him awake that night. That his father had praised Pablo, that he had seen him and knew his whereabouts, was not so important as knowing that the little Zácaro might be sharing God with him. This thought was unbearable, terrible. Until he felt the proximity of his brother, he had never realized that God also existed for others. Once again, it tortured him to think that his brother might look like him. But now, he did not want anyone to look like him. Instead, he was ready to pray for Pablo Zácaro to be sinful and earthy like Juan Senior, like Salome, like everybody. So unlike him. It was then that he became aware of his pride. But he could not help it, he just could not. He had fostered it so much during those years of solitude!

He realized that he could not live without seeing Pablo. He had to meet him, touch his hands and face, listen to his voice, and look into his eyes. When the sun came up, Juan went out to the country to search for him. The people were winnowing straw. He went toward the threshing floor where the Zácaros usually worked. A warm wind was blowing, and Juan climbed the hill slowly so that they would not see him too soon.

The threshing floor was glowing like an ember. Straw flew about in sparkling swarms. Salome was sifting the wheat, her naked brown arms shining in the sun. She was talking with her sister at the top of her voice and laughing. There were a number of children on the threshing floor: some were playing with the dog and others were winnowing with small wooden tridents. Juan's chest filled with fire and his heart pounded like a hammer on an anvil. Then one of the older children noticed him and, with a snicker, pointed him out to the others. Shortly, the mocking song burst out: "Big head, big head,

40

poor little big head . . ." The others on the threshing floor could barely suppress their laughter and pretended not to notice. Juan Junior stood still, watching them. The dog also began to bark at him. Seeing his impassiveness, the children's song became livelier. They gathered together and slowly approached him in a group. The last to join the crowd was the smallest one. A lively dark-haired boy who, without saying anything, bent down to pick up a stone. He hurled it at Juan with a primitive, cruel little laugh. It seemed that he already knew that he was attacking the master's son. Then a woman's voice cried out: "Pablo! Come here, you devil!" It was Salome. The child who threw the stone put his hands in his pockets and looked at Juan, smiling with innocent defiance. Juan Junior stared at the boy, his look piercing him like a sword. The child was tall and strong for his age. Shiny locks of black hair fell over his eyes. His teeth, white and sharp, were gleaming. He looked like a wolf cub.

Juan backed up slowly, bowing his head. Already he was captured. Imprisoned there forever, beside that little cub of a man, loving him and fearing him at the same time. He had already begun to love and hate him in a confused way early on the morning when he was born, lying there on that same threshing floor. His feelings, which until that moment had kept him distant, changed completely. He realized that he was very close to men, closer to men than to anything or anybody. As close as the earth to water. He would not be going back to school anymore. He would stay there, near his brother. His pride became human, became blood to him. He must conquer him. He had to best Pablo Zácaro.

The dog followed him at a distance, barking.

6

"I am a despicable miser."

The proper grandson of the moneylender. But Juan Senior, with his spendthrift ways, was to blame for that. During the period when his father was housebound because of the accident, young Juan had begun to study him carefully. Juan Senior could not bear the forced inactivity, and so, in order to entertain himself, he devised foolish distractions that irritated his quiet, withdrawn son. Juan Junior, who loved stillness, secrecy, and silence, had to put up with the shouting and violence of the old man.

One day, his father instructed the servants to put his armchair out on the balcony overlooking the patio. Then he ordered them to serve wine to the laborers when they came home from the fields, as much wine as they could drink down there on the golden flagstones. He himself would preside over the party from the balcony, pitcher in hand. He just could not get along without other people, even if it meant attending the rowdy parties of his servants. It was late September. The men who came back from sowing the fields got thoroughly drunk around a large bonfire in the patio, while up on the balcony their master sang in a raucous voice. The flagstones were covered with green bottles, and spilled wine shone red in the firelight. Although it was beginning to get cold, everybody was sweating as though it were the middle of summer. When the sky began to brighten, men were leaning on the columns or lying on the ground snoring. From his window, Juan Junior had been watching the scene below. He told himself: "When they work for me, I'll dominate them with silence and order. I won't be extravagant because it's not good. I'll moderate their lives." Because everything in his father was excessive, large, and violent, young Juan reacted by becoming stingy, small, and miserly. His father oppressed with his extravagance; he would rule with his fists closed, by squeezing.

"We've been given so much. If we feel like it, we can afford to throw our money out the window and spread the wealth around," his father said. And just as Juan Senior had rebelled against Grandfather Juan, so Juan Junior reacted to his father. While watching the drunks in the patio, he observed their blatant disrespect as they made jokes about their master, who pretended not to hear or perhaps did not understand. Young Juan thought: "When I'm in charge, they won't talk back, and everything will be in its place, peaceful and orderly." Just then he thought of Pablo Zácaro and of the time when the boy would be working for him. His blood boiled.

He would watch his brother from afar, like a spy, hiding in the shadows or among the trees. He observed how young and lively he was, and – so much like his father – unusually generous in that land of poor wretches. Pablo shared his bread with the dogs, and he did so in the reasonable, fair manner of someone older and wiser. Juan had heard him speak only once or twice, but he noted that he had a clear voice and used concise, direct words, without the usual complaining or angry exclamations typical of the region. Nor did he share the wild shyness of the other children in Artámila. Pablo's features reminded him of Salome. Yet there was something in his tiny person, in his manner of walking, that made Juan think: "He doesn't look like anybody else." His steps were firm, and he often went about with his hands in his pockets, unhurriedly, like a little man. Although he was somewhat indifferent to others' feelings, he was one of those children who inspired affection in others. Without even trying, without even smiling. Among the peasant women who worked with Salome, the little Zácaro boy moved in an aureole of harsh love, of indulgence for his mischievous ways. Juan could not understand it. Even the dogs followed him about, and rarely did the other boys hit him. Nevertheless, Pablo did not care for displays of affection, and on one occasion, Juan saw him push Salome away when she tried to kiss him. Like a wild animal, he would not allow himself to be caressed or even touched.

One day, while his father was in the patio, they saw the little Zácaro boy go by the fence. He was headed toward the river with a mastiff puppy under each arm. Juan Senior was walking again with the help of a crutch. When he saw Pablo, he rushed as fast as he could to the gate. Juan Junior followed in his shadow. As Pablo was about to disappear around the corner, his father called out: "Zácaro!"

The boy turned around but did not approach them. Juan Senior gazed at him, with that radiant smile that sometimes lit up his face. It seemed that he had just made a big effort, as if he had not really wanted to call him but was not able to contain himself. Now he did not even know what to say to him. Pablo turned around again, to go on his way. Once again his father could not keep quiet and called him: "Come here!" The child obeyed without shyness.

"What kind of mutts are those?" he asked. Saying nothing, Pablo handed him one of the two puppies. Young Juan noted that his father's face turned red and that he did not know what to do with the whelp in his hands. "Where are you taking them?"

"Down to the river," said Pablo.

"Well, look. . . , I'll buy this one from you, you hear, boy? He's going to be the prettiest mastiff in all of Artámila, and you were going to drown him! No way! I'll keep him."

"He's ugly," answered Pablo with aplomb. "And he's going to die without his mother."

"Shut up!" responded Juan Senior violently. "What the hell do

44

you know, you little brat? If I want to buy him, I know what I'm doing. How much do you want for him?"

Pablo just looked at him without responding. Quickly, his father took a silver coin from his pocket and gave it to him. With the puppy under his arm, he went back into the house. Pablo looked at the coin that shone in the palm of his hand and then bit it with his wolflike teeth, as he had seen his mother do on the days when the ironmonger came to the village. Juan Junior had never seen his brother so close up. Pablo's hands were big, hard, and his skin a rough brown like Salome's. Bluish black forelocks fell over his eyebrows, and his nose was short and wide with flaring nostrils like those of a hunting animal. He continued on his way, and Juan followed him with feelings of both admiration and rancor. His father had never given him any money.

It was cold, winter was coming, but Pablo Zácaro wore only a ripped shirt and blue trousers. He did not seem to be cold, however. Juan noted his brother's elbows and knees, which were apple-red in color. He, on the other hand, was shivering in his leather jacket. How was it that Pablo's skin glowed and his black hair shone when he spent his days working on the land, which dirties everything? How smooth and hard he was, like a clean young tree. Juan, on the contrary, always seemed weak and dirty, with his nose full of snot. Suddenly, he quickened his pace and grabbed Pablo by the arm.

"Hey, you thief . . ." he said. His voice sounded deep and tremulous. Years later that voice would disconcert Dingo, the puppeteer. Pablo looked at him then, and Juan saw his eyes up close. He had large pupils, spherical and transparent, like black grapes. There inside, light was transformed into a burning wine. No, they were not a child's eyes. Juan's voice died in his throat.

"I'm not a thief," said Pablo, quickly extricating himself from Juan's grasp. He was neither angry nor fearful. What a strange serenity there was in that creature. His voice was like his steps, with the pure straightness of an arrow or a stalk of wheat.

45

"Yes, you are a thief, because that dog's going to die, and you kept the money."

"Well, take it!" Pablo gave him the coin. Before Juan had time to say anything, Pablo was headed toward the river with the other puppy under his arm.

It had rained the night before, and the muddy red water flowed over the stones with a quiet murmur. Juan leaned against the trunk of a tree, squeezing the silver coin in his hand. It burned as if it would melt in his fist. He had a lump in his throat, and his painful urge to cry felt like needles stuck in his neck. Meanwhile, Pablo, indifferent to the storm in Juan's chest, grabbed the puppy by his hind legs and with a stone hit him hard on the head. A weak little cry was heard. Pablo's cheeks were splattered with crimson drops. Cleaning the blood off of his face with his forearm, he threw the little dog into the water. Pablo waited, hands in his pockets, until it disappeared down-river in the swollen current. Then, quickly, he began his climb up the slope to the woods, whose ground was covered with yellow leaves.

Autumn was shedding its foliage among the black trunks; there was something indomitable, spirited, in the figure of the little boy. Juan still followed him, obstinately, not knowing what he wanted from him.

They reached the game warden's cabin. That land also belonged to the Juans. At the door of the hut, sitting on the floor, was a boy around fourteen years old, with a cat in his lap. An orange cat with stripes on his back.

A few steps ahead of him, Pablo called out, "Dingo!" The older boy raised his head. "I went to drown the puppies, and the master bought one from me. But this guy says that the little dog is going to die right away, so he kept the money for himself."

Juan shrank back and thought to himself: "So the puppies belonged to this other fellow, who sent Pablo to drown them."

Dingo stood up. Still petting the cat, he glared at Juan, who began to back away. Dingo was at least four years older than he, a big, tall

46

boy. Juan was afraid, as always when he expected to be beaten. Whenever his father was going to whip him, he would shake like a leaf even before the first lash.

"So you kept the money," said Dingo, squinting his eyes. (Even then he was theatrical. All the children of Artámila were fascinated with the effect of his mimicry, the changing shades of his voice, and his slapstick humor.)

"The dog wasn't worth it. . . , he wasn't worth it. . . ," said Juan, trembling with fear. Quickly Dingo pushed him, and Juan fell to the ground, his back on the carpet of dead leaves that covered the forest floor. Beneath Juan's chin, Dingo's big fists grabbed the lapels of his jacket and shook him.

"He wasn't worth it, he wasn't worth it. . . ," mimicked Dingo. "So, what business is this of yours? Who the hell are you to be keeping the money. . . ?"

All of a sudden, Dingo's expression changed. His hands weakened their grip, and he let them fall softly. The striped cat had jumped up on his shoulder and was rubbing against his head. Dingo stared at Juan with amazement: "Listen. . . ," he began to say in a very different tone of voice. "You wouldn't happen to be the master's son?"

Juan nodded weakly. Now he would hit him. He would surely hit him harder or spit in his face. How all the village children hated him!

But this time he was wrong. Dingo helped him up and brushed the leaves off his back. His hair was still full of twigs, and his lips were trembling. Dingo noticed it and said: "Come on, you're not going to start crying now? Can't you see that I didn't know who you were? Since you never come down to the plaza or go out to the fields. . . , and I'm always in the forest!"

Juan dried a tear from his cheek with the back of his hand.

But Dingo would never know why he was crying. Juan looked at the game warden's son. He looked at him for a long time, with his head raised, since he barely reached Dingo's waist.

47

"Take it, it's yours," he finally said, putting the silver coin in Dingo's hand. Then he turned around and plunged into the woods, taking the path down to the house of the Juans.

Dingo saw him disappear, somewhat surprised. Then he bit the coin, just like Pablo and Salome. There was no doubt: it was good.

When Juan reached the house, he went up to his room and closed himself in, as if someone were pursuing him. The walls were very white and bare. Only a black cross was hanging over the bed. A breeze blew the curtain, and on the hill of the Northwest Cemetery, the black poplars bent in the wind. Never had he felt so cold inside, not even during winter nights. The room looked more naked than ever, completely bare. Yes, he was miserly, very miserly, because he had nothing. He looked at the palms of his hands. One end of his scarf, frayed and slack, fell down to his waist. He heard a dog bark and looked out the window. The stable boy was playing with one of the dogs in the patio. Not even the dogs liked him. He did not even have an orange cat who would jump up on his shoulder, like Dingo, the game warden's son. Why hadn't Dingo hit him? Why hadn't he made fun of his sickly, clumsy body? He had not called him knock-kneed, or big head, or drooling fool. No. He had not said anything like that. And he had brushed off the dead leaves that were stuck to his jacket.

With a strange fury, he opened the collar of his shirt. The medallion stood out against his pale yellow skin, and the light shone on its little engraved cross. He then asked God to save him the wait. He prayed for Him to leave his useless body in the ground, deep in the ground with all its worms and ants and flowers. He begged God to spare his having to grow up, having to continue growing and leaving blank spaces between things and himself. Growing, growing into himself, and burning years like torches . . . Now there was no corner of the room without light. Before setting, the sun had flooded the room with its rays. Everything was lit up, desperately, the four corners of the room intensely red. In the middle, Juan Medinao felt like

48

a mirror of everything that surrounded him; he saw how all of the gratuitous extravagance of life was reflected on him. The money-lender's grandson wanted to save himself the trouble of living.

At that moment, he heard a whistle over the sound of the wind. A large golden leaf drifted above the patio, turning circles. He thought at first that it might be a shepherd's whistle, but then he heard it again, close by.

It was Dingo, perched on the stockade fence, making signals for him to come down. He had come to look for him! To look for him . . .

He quickly ran downstairs. At eleven years old, a child can go without transition from the darkest desperation to almost painful joy. Dingo was calling him. Dingo, who neither made fun of him nor hit him.

Dingo looked at him with a meek and wheedling expression. He only wanted to chat awhile, he said, as if it were the most natural thing. Little did Dingo know that nobody, absolutely nobody, ever bothered to chat awhile with Juan Junior. They sat on the ground, and Dingo demonstrated the charms of Perico, the striped cat. He had taught him to jump through a small wicker hoop, to dance on his hind legs, to play ball, and to pass a tiny plate held between his teeth begging for a nickel. He also had made a little pointed hat of paper for the cat's head. "I charge the village children a few coppers to see this," Dingo let slip at the end of the show. Juan Medinao shook his head slowly: "I don't have any money."

"Come on!" answered Dingo, his eyes sparkling. "Your father must have some, because if he doesn't, what is this?" From out of his pocket he took the silver coin, which shone weakly because the sun had almost set.

"But I don't have any money now. . . ," repeated Juan disappointedly.

"No, no, man, I'm not going to charge you anything," answered Dingo with a magnanimous expression.

Juan thought he was dreaming. How was it possible that this big boy was showing him signs of friendship? He did not understand it then. Dingo's masks were still unknown to him; even those that were made of clay and fell apart at night.

On the following two afternoons, at the same time, Dingo returned. He brought not only Perico, but also some tiny dolls, which he had made from walnuts, painting their faces with blackberry juice. With strings he made them jump and dance and even fight with each other. All those little figures appeared out of the pockets of his jacket, like people looking over balconies. Dingo smelled of sawdust and green wood. Juan's admiration for him swelled like a flooded river.

Then, unexpectedly, the game warden appeared and grabbed Dingo by the ear. He had been looking for him, and he told his son that he was a lazy good-for-nothing and that he should be digging in the garden behind the cabin at that very moment.

"Every day it's the same thing!" he yelled as he dragged Dingo away. "You probably think that you're going to be living off other people forever! Well, I'm going to teach you a lesson. . . ! So you think we're living in the lap of luxury!"

Off he went saying other such things, calling him a damned loafer. He was furious. Dingo held his two hands over his head, while the man kept hitting him with his cane. On the road, the puppets fell out of his pockets, and Juan, following at a distance, picked them up as if they were treasures. When they reached the cabin in the woods, there, next to the garden where Dingo had not wanted to work, the game warden took off his belt and beat his son. Every blow seemed to rebound off Juan's back.

When the game warden had gone away, Juan approached his friend and sat down beside him. The cat, who had fled when the beating began, returned now, meowing hypocritically. Dingo lay face down in the dead leaves, his head hidden in his arms; he trembled slightly but did not complain. The blows had torn his shirt.

50

"He always does the same thing," he said after a while. "He wants me to work . . ."

"My father beats me too," said Juan Medinao. "As hard as yours beats you."

Dingo raised his head, surprised. "Does he also want you to work?"

"No. . . ," Juan remained thoughtful. It wasn't for that. His father beat him when he was afraid. Or if Juan misaimed the gun during a shooting lesson in the patio. Or when his father asked him to tell a story, and Juan Junior could not come up with the words. "He beats me for other reasons," he explained.

Brusquely, Dingo unbuttoned his shirt and showed him his back. Juan knew well those red strips of skin that would slowly swell up and burn like fire. In turn, Juan showed him a scar on his cheek.

"It's a belt buckle," he said.

"And when you were in school, did the friars beat you?"

"Yes, but only on my face and with their hands."

"Yeah, just like women!"

Dingo's lips were dry and pale. He put on his jacket, carefully. In his eyes there was a painful, pleading look: that meek complaint of those accustomed to beatings.

"God damn them! Why can't they just leave us alone?"

"Look, Dingo, I picked up your puppets along the road."

Seated on the ground, and instead of digging in the garden, they began to piece together the heads and legs of the walnut dolls. They worked in silence, absorbed in their task, when all of a sudden, a strange sound carried on the wind made Dingo perk up his head. He looked like a dog sniffing game.

"Look, there, over there, Juan Medinao!" he cried. He jumped up and began running like a madman.

There, at the top of the hill, appeared a wagon of traveling performers. It was making its way slowly down the road.

"Run, Juan Medinao! Run, the gypsies are coming!"

They went running to the plaza, having forgotten all about beatings and puppets. At the cabin, Perico, with his back arched, jumped up onto the windowsill.

Inevitably, by following the road, the wagon would end up in the plaza. When Juan and Dingo got there, the village children had already discovered the arrival of the puppeteers. They buzzed in a swarm like bees. The little Zácaro boy was off to the side, hands in his pockets. Instead of looking at the hill, he watched the other children. Juan thought: "Pablo Zácaro has already bought his ticket and has begun to watch the show."

"They'll probably have trained dogs," Dingo explained enthusiastically to the crowd of youngsters, who listened with their mouths open. As he spoke of those fabulous dogs, Perico's exploits seemed to pale. Dingo's head and shoulders stood up over the crowd. The undug garden was now forgotten. The other boys of Dingo's age had been helping their fathers in the fields for some time now.

The wagon was arriving. On the driver's seat sat a boy beside a man with a large black moustache and a cross expression. The children ran toward them, shouting. With a thunderous voice the man yelled, "Out of my way!"

He told them to clear aside since he had no intention of staying in Lower Artámila. They were going to pass through the village, to leave it behind with its wild, impatient children. But the children, who did not understand, stood quietly in a group, obstructing his path. Only by flicking his whip over their heads did the man finally disperse them.

With a plaintive and disillusioned voice, one child still cried: "Stay on, stay!"

"They're going away . . ." said Dingo.

His shoulders now had the defeated shape of childish despair. It was as if the puppeteers were taking away half of his life. The other children appeared to be crestfallen as well, with a bitterness and fatigue beyond their years. But none of them watched the wagon go off with Dingo's eyes, those imploring wide-set eyes. The wagon crossed the heart of the village and continued on its way to another richer land. Only Pablo Zácaro watched it with the expression of a reflective and dispassionate spectator. Since they were all so quiet, the squeaking of the wheels going off in the distance could be heard clearly.

"They're going away," repeated Dingo. And Juan smiled with melancholy. He knew very well: it was like everything, as always. They were going away.

The children disappeared around corners, quietly. Only Juan and Dingo still followed the wagon, not yet resigned to seeing it go. They chased the yellow cloud of dust stirred up by the wheels.

Outside the village, they finally stopped. Dingo sat down at the foot of a solitary black poplar that grew beside the road. It was the last tree in Lower Artámila. A cold wind made them shrink inside their jackets. The wagon, in the distance now, was lost in the evening's darkness. Dingo said dismally: "I'm leaving . . . I'm going to run away and I'll never return."

He said that he would run off with a wagon like that one, and he would travel through towns, through all the towns in the world. Listening to him, Juan smiled again, sadly. He also knew that. He knew that, inevitably, Dingo would leave him one day.

Suddenly, Dingo pointed to him with his finger: "And you too, Juan Medinao! We'll go together! Let them stay here, lashing the wind with their belts!"

He stood up, and together they slowly returned to the village. Dingo put his arm over Juan's shoulders, and as they walked along, he talked incessantly about plans for their future. Once in a while he would stop in order to give a confidential tone to his voice.

"You see this?" he said, taking the silver coin out of his pocket. "This is just the beginning of everything we're going to save, you and I."

They had to save a lot of money, the two of them.

Silver coins. Juan Senior always carried silver coins in his pockets. They said good-bye with a strong handshake. That night, Juan Junior felt that he had grown up.

With great solemnity, they buried the first coin at the foot of the black poplar along the road, in the hope of saving a large sum. Dingo said that they would have to buy a wagon, supplies, and paint. Perico also seemed to be in on the secret. At times, when he saw them together, talking mysteriously, he would arch his back and howl like a tiger. He was also one of the gang, and in his name, they buried a pile of small change, the fruits of his latest performances.

Every afternoon, while his father was napping, Juan Junior would check the pockets of his jacket, left hanging on the coat rack. It was easy to know when his father was coming by the sound of his crutch thumping on the floor tiles. Later on in the evening, he would get together with Dingo, and the two of them would take care so that no one would see them as they took the main road out to the poplar tree.

Nearly a month went by. One day, his father surprised him. He had just stopped using the crutch, so young Juan had not heard him coming.

At first his father was not so angry. He called him a thief and a coward. But he had been more annoyed when his son had misaimed the gun in the patio. However, when his father asked him what he spent the money on, Juan Junior did not respond. Then his father became enraged. He hit him hard across the face and dragged him by the arm to the stable.

In the patio Dingo waited, hiding behind a column. As he passed by, Juan Junior saw the pleading look in Dingo's eyes and thought: "No, I won't talk." And he said nothing.

His father whipped him more than ten times with a leather strap; young Juan clenched his teeth. He knew that Dingo was out there, listening to everything. When the beating finally stopped and he was left stretched out on the straw, a painful, rebellious pride comforted him like wine. His fury vented, his father looked at him and felt compassion: "He's not strong," he said to himself. "Anything could break him." The child's skinny yellow back trembled like a dying bird. The marks of the strap were becoming inflamed. "Oh, now I know," thought Juan Senior, with sudden clarity. "He's a goddamned miser, like his grandfather. Surely he's been robbing me because he doesn't dare ask for money, and he saves it and piles it up in a hollowed-out rafter . . . Just like his grandfather, the cursed miser." He left with mixed feelings of pity and contempt for the boy and with the quiet resentment that came over him every time he thought of his father.

As soon as he saw him leave, Dingo jumped through the stable window and knelt down beside Juan. He had brought a wet handkerchief and spread it over his friend's back.

"Don't worry. When we leave, this will be over. Nobody will ever raise a hand to us again. We'll see the ocean, and Madrid, and we'll buy five dogs who will learn to dance . . ."

It was on these occasions that Juan would shut his eyes and listen to him speak of escapades. Secretly, he had always believed it to be impossible. But it was so wonderful to listen to Dingo, the liar, talk on and on about those escapades. Dingo was never very precise about where he would live, as he went on about his fantastic plans for the future.

From that day forth, Juan Senior allotted him a small weekly sum of money, all of which he added to increase the savings under the black poplar. Young Juan was devoured by an obsession for collecting silver coins. Sometimes, at night, he felt tempted to go out to the road, to lift up the stone that covered the treasure, to touch it, and to contemplate it under the moonlight. In fact, running away did not interest him in the same way as it did Dingo. What he wanted was Dingo's friendship, the plans of his absurd fantasy, and the confidence of their secrets. To have this, there or somewhere else, made no difference to him. He had to have Dingo's masks close by, his lies that, like wine, went to his head and numbed him to all else.

55

A year passed by. One night, a troupe of traveling actors came to town in a splendid wagon.

It was the month of August, when the field chores were most arduous. A perfectly round moon illuminated the plaza. The laborers returned from their toil exhausted, and everyone thought that the wagon would soon be on its way. It was possibly the most beautiful wagon that had ever come to the Artámilas.

Dingo and Juan, with hands in their pockets, were leaning against the wall of a laborer's hut. Their shadows extended across the fiery earth of the deserted plaza. They watched the wagon arrive, its little windows lit up by a flickering yellow light.

In the middle of the plaza it stopped. Dingo, seeing that it was not just passing on through the town, stretched out his hand, still and open like a fan. One could almost hear his heart throbbing in the quiet atmosphere. The wagon had three horses and was as big as a house. Its gaudily painted door opened, and some hands set a ladder to the ground. There was light in the wagon, candlelight, like the light in a storybook palace. A man emerged. He was big and fat, with a green frock coat and a trumpet in his hand. Immediately, children and dogs began to jump out of the wagon. At least eight children, who turned somersaults on the ground and said hello with their arms open. They may have been dressed in rags, but they were colorful tatters: shreds of cloth that floated with the rhythm of their movements, like trumpet music.

Dingo was bedazzled; his eyes sparkled with tears of amazement. He approached them and stood in the middle of their pirouettes and music, gazing at the man with his mouth open. On his shoulder, Perico seemed to be electrified as well.

The troupe had quickly organized its whirl through town. They began sticking up posters on trees and huts. Posters that in their impatience they never read. Posters whose announcements would remain unknown forever.

Dingo then writhed on the ground, like a wounded bull. His callused bare feet stirred up little red clouds of dust from the plaza. His arms were also open, and Perico went down his back like a circus number. Juan would never forget it: the light from the open wagon divided him into two colors, like a strange harlequin, a harlequin made up of mud and blood.

"They're staying, Juan Medinao, they're staying!"

It was a miracle. It was like one of Dingo's fantasies, one of Dingo's lies. The children marched in file between the huts, announcing the spectacle. The last one, who was small and deformed, played the drum monotonously. Their voices, which sang a rhythmical march, were lost in the corners with a diffuse, ghostly echo. Juan Medinao, in the grips of an inexplicable fear, ran off toward his house. Why wasn't he happy? Why did he feel a vague apprehension enter through his pores, like a cold sweat? Dingo, with his eyes on his temples and split in two by the light, looked to him like a diabolical doll. Suddenly, Juan remembered that he had been stealing money, that he had been robbing his father, right before going to Central Artámila to receive his first communion and listen to the bells. Juan Senior was not at home. As soon as he recovered completely from his accident, he resumed his habit of leaving the house for long periods.

Juan Medinao peered out of his window. The moonlight gilded the Northwest Cemetery, and he could hear the noise of the acrobats and the dogs barking. Like the dead, he was numb and deaf to happiness, letting the moon slide over him imperceptibly, in vague anguish. But Dingo had gone looking for him and was whistling in the patio, as he did every afternoon.

The show took place in the plaza itself. Only the young people attended, those who did not succumb to fatigue and sleepiness. And the very little children who still robbed swallows' nests and stole green fruit. They sat on the ground, forming a wide circle around the acrobats.

The man in the frock coat had stuck in the ground four torches, which illuminated the performance. The show was made up of the eight children, who dressed in the wagon and jumped down to the red earth to form human towers, turn somersaults, and sing songs with the sound of rain. The smallest one, who looked like an idiot, accompanied the numbers with a distant drumbeat, a monotonous and haunting echo. He must have been a deaf-mute because he would stop playing only when the man gestured to him. The dogs wore hats and ruffs, and the big man carried a little yellow whip, so tiny that it looked ridiculous. That man in the green frock coat, with his wig and wide smile, seemed sinister to Juan. What terrified him most were the man's teeth, which reminded him of the chipped stucco on the graveyard wall. His skin was white, as if made of plaster. He stood there and shouted at the children acrobats through his fixed smile and cracked his little whip in the air. There was something in the entire show that smelled of death, of rotten flowers. From under the slippers of the little tumblers, the red dust of Artámila rose like furious smoke, up to the moon. A wet and sticky sadness drenched young Juan. The fat man's eyes appeared to be empty, like two cavities. And his voice was cavernous. His expressions of exaggerated courtesy seemed so affected to the audience of Artámila that it provoked a coarse, derisive roar. In response, the fat man bowed and accepted the mockery as applause. Juan then noticed his hands, which were large, brutal, and as hard as rocks. It hurt to look at them. Instinctively he turned his eyes to the childrens' little bodies, to their skinny arms and legs, whose muscles were freakishly overdeveloped. The children's bodies reminded him of August sprouts that break underfoot because the sun has burned them too soon. They all wore powder and held their faces frozen with rigid smiles, while drops of sweat poured down their cheeks. How miserable everything had turned all of a sudden! How tinny and garish their ornaments! Their colorful tatters were rags, and their thinness was hunger. Next to that old wooden wagon, Dingo's walnut puppets painted with blackberry juice would have shone like flowers. It was no splendid wagon: it was a big coffin full of maggots

58

and woodworm. Juan shivered. He sat behind Dingo, and the nape of his friend's neck looked black, with the motionlessness of wonder, of reverie. This was the last time that Juan saw Dingo as a child, burning with dreams.

Juan began moving away, furtively retreating from the plaza. Dingo's head was haloed in the torches' fire. Fleeing the scene, he clambered uphill toward his house. Once or twice he turned to see the plaza growing smaller and smaller until it looked like the center of a toy village. The drum, on the other hand, resonated louder and louder in his head, although the voices were lost.

All of a sudden, he found himself standing in front of the Zácaros' hut. And, as on that other morning, it was Rosa who came out and saw him.

"Go on, get out of here," she said. "Our boy has got the measles, and you don't want to catch them right before your first communion. Run along now!"

Juan spent the entire next day at home. He prayed and begged God's forgiveness for having stolen from his father. In the afternoon, he waited in vain for Dingo's whistle and slept uneasily that night, his sleep disturbed by the sound of an imaginary drumbeat.

On the morning of the second day, a deep premonition led him to the dug-up earth at the foot of the black poplar. Since there was no wind, not a speck of dust blurred the hardness of the deserted and endless road that led far away. Dingo and Perico had vanished, like everything else.

7

"I had a brother. I speak of him now because he determined my life and my sins. I don't blame him, but ever since I first knew him, I have lived in an emotional hell full of envy and anger. And also love. This love has been my greatest sin. It is still my burden and wherever I go, I will carry it with me."

Pablo Zácaro became a man. One day, one year, he appeared as if after a long sleep.

Juan Medinao, in the patio, was watching the laborers return from the fields. Suddenly he saw his brother in a wagon full of straw, glowing like fire in the sunlight. Juan Medinao, who oversaw the arrival of his workers, felt as if, all at once, the past years were whirling before his eyes. Only yesterday, it seemed, Rosa had sent him away so that he would not catch the measles. Only yesterday, Juan Senior had given Pablo a silver coin in exchange for the mastiff puppy.

The mastiff, at his side, was now old. And his father, who had cared for that puppy with an uncharacteristic concern so that he would not die, was himself now dead. Like so many winters, like so many words.

"How old is Pablo Zácaro, Salome's son?" Juan asked his foreman that night.

"Maybe eighteen . . ."

The whole country was asleep. Juan Medinao, with his shirt open at his chest and his feet bare like when he was a child, went outside, under the moon. In the ghostly atmosphere he walked through the harvested wheat fields. Sheaves were piled on the ground, waiting to be brought to the threshing floor. Juan gazed over the land with a strange thirst. He came to the forest. The game warden's cabin was dark; Dingo and Perico now belonged to the departed, to the nonliving, like his twenty-three years. What had he done since the death of his father? He stopped to think about it. The harvests had increased twofold. He had saved more than money: he had spared Artámila parties and drunks. There were no more harvest celebrations in the patio. Now he dressed like the other peasants. There were no more queens of the harvest, no pink-and-green dresses. Juan Medinao had appeared incorporeal in the eyes of his people. He never went looking for their women. He never got drunk. He walked eight kilometers every Sunday to the parish church to hear mass. He could not bear the thought that his laborers might discover that he was a man, earthy like them. He kept himself distant, alone, living like a novice of a private religion. That night, standing like another tree in the forest, with twenty-three years less of life, he tried to explain time to himself. On such a night, his father had died of apoplexy. Juan Junior had sat up with him as was his duty, with respect, without love. And he had accompanied him to the Northwest Cemetery, where they hid his livid body deep in the ground so that no one would smell his blood as it turned black. Any day, any night, they would also bury him, Juan Medinao, among the bones and roots. He would pass on to time, to the enigma of time gone by. With his voice, with his memories, with his hunger for God, and with his fear.

A strong warm wind swept over the village. Juan Medinao continued wandering among the trees, with the dry windstorm whipping his skin. Pablo Zácaro was now eighteen years old. Eighteen years.

Once, long ago, a dog's blood had splattered his face, yet how clean, how icy he had appeared among the flames of the straw that morning. Pablo Zácaro was wearing a white shirt. The sleeves were too short, and his arms, brown as if rubbed with walnut juice, stuck out of the unbuttoned cuffs.

Juan's thirst led him on, like a premonition. He had crossed the forest and, reaching its edge, where the trees stopped near the craggy ridge of the mountain, he paused, still as a statue. Pablo Zácaro was there working by the moonlight. In the silence of the night he heard the sound of a shovel and the murmur of water from a nearby spring. He saw then that Pablo was building walls of stone and earth, like those of a shepherd's hut.

"What are you building?" Juan said out loud.

Pablo turned around. With his arm, he wiped the sweat from his brow. "A house," he replied.

For the first time, they looked at each other as men.

"Who has given you permission? You're on my land."

"This is not your land. There is the edge of the forest, and this ground is not yours."

He threw the shovel to the side and, approaching the spring, bent over to drink. So he had been going there at night to make himself a hut, because during the day he had to work in the fields for Juan Medinao.

"So what do you want this house for, you fool? Don't you have one already in the village? I don't even charge you rent for the house where you live! It's one of the best in Artámila."

"I want a house of my own, made with my own hands. Ever since I was a child, I have been thinking about this. Every man should build a house for himself."

Then, a violent, absurd anger took hold of Juan Medinao. An intense fury, strange and unjustified. His brother's presence, his voice tore something under his skin. Something unknown burst in his chest, like a smashed idol. He felt like throwing his soil on top of him, all of his soil. He wanted to shut him up, burying him under the dirt, covering Pablo's mouth with his land. He wanted him dead, his flesh rotting in the dust. In his forest, among the roots of the oak trees, feeding the branches with the sap of his body.

Juan left quickly. A dark premonition made him shiver despite the heat of the night.

On the following days, while Pablo was working in the field, Juan returned more than once to see how the house was coming along. Though crude and roughly built, there was something alive about it, something that came directly from the hands of a man. He did not dare to touch it.

Two months later, on a Sunday morning, when he had just returned from Central Artámila, a maid came to tell him: "The laborers want to talk to you, Juan Medinao."

Immediately he realized that for the last thirteen years, since the day when Pablo had thrown a stone at him, he had lived waiting for that moment.

In fact, his brother led the committee. Pablo Zácaro had barely been able to go to school. He was a peasant, yet his words were so powerful, so just that Juan could only envy him. Juan had yet to hear him, but he knew what Pablo was going to say. Where did his brother get that serene strength, that peaceful certainty? His power lay in the fact that he walked a straight road. Pablo Zácaro knew what he wanted, and he moved toward his goals without hesitation. Even as a child, his brother had made Juan think of straight arrows, of stalks of wheat, or of hard roads without bends. Even if he were mistaken, Pablo would see his mistake through until the end. Didn't the fool realize that he was advancing toward death and that all his strength was worthless? Anger slid into his soul, like molten lava. Pablo Zácaro had become a man, simple and forthright. He did not need school or religion, love or understanding in order to advance. And now he was coming straight to Juan Medinao, to his heart, to his forehead, like an unavoidable bullet.

Pablo Zácaro stepped across the golden flagstones of the patio. Behind him, the three foremen seemed unimportant and indecisive.

"Juan Medinao, we want you to increase our daily wage."

Juan looked at the ground. His brother's feet were bare, and their copper color stood out in the golden dust.

"Who's in charge of this?"

"Everybody," responded Pablo.

The three foremen became noticeably more hesitant. Juan's voice came out quavering and hoarse: "You three, leave! You, Zácaro, stay!"

"No." There they stood, still as trees.

"All right then," said Juan, controlling his anger. "Why do you want a raise? You don't need anything. I always make sure that you lack for nothing."

"We are the worst-paid laborers in the region."

"Imbecile! You ignorant fool! Tell me, what is it that you need? What do you need money for? Any worker from the city would love to be in your shoes, and you dare protest! Have you ever gone hungry?"

"No, I have never gone hungry."

"What more do you want?"

Pablo smiled. It was the first time that Juan ever saw him smile as a man. He still had those wolf teeth, white and shining like knives.

"My own land. And if I die of hunger, it will be my own fault."

Juan Medinao squeezed his hands together; his palms were wet. His voice was deep, soft, and stealthy: "In Lower Artámila the land is mine. Anyone who doesn't want to work can leave."

"No one will work on your land, Juan Medinao. No one, until you change your mind."

They left slowly. The three foremen, not raising their heads, stumbled into the fence as they left the patio. Only Pablo left peacefully, stepping firmly and softly with his bare feet.

"Time is going to drag for him now," Juan said to himself, tighten-

64

ing his fists. He thinks he's the first person to say that . . . And he's going directly to the bottom of a grave with all his mistakes. Like so many before him and so many after him. As long as I live, there's going to be peace. Peace and quiet, while I wait. I have enough to live on without them. My wheat will just have to rot in silence . . ."

Just like that, without ever having heard of strikes, Pablo Zácaro organized the first one against his brother.

The sun burned down over the grass and the wheat. At first, the men held strong, and hunger spread throughout Lower Artámila.

Juan Medinao calculated his riches. He could live for the rest of his life there in the house, within its bare walls, surrounded by his dead fields. He would walk among his oak trees as he waited. The fruits of his orchard would be lost; they would fall to the ground and then would sprout up again desolately. Summer was coming to an end.

Sometimes Juan Medinao would see women and children toiling in their miserable little gardens outside his jurisdiction. The men went to the other Artámilas seeking work. The house of the Juans was now full of echoes, echoes of its solitude and silence. No straw gleamed between the flagstones of the patio, which were as bare as in winter. Only the women who worked in his household would cross occasionally in front of his window in their black clothes. During the afternoons, the deep red facade of the house took on a somber shade. Juan noticed how his sense of peace was torn to shreds; his peace was but a wormy, dead lie. There was only silence in his house and on his land because there was turmoil in his soul. Pablo Zácaro, on the other hand, lived in true serenity, without fury or rapture.

The time for sowing was approaching. Juan Medinao bumped into his shadow on all the walls and fled from the forest. His suit was dirtier and more wrinkled than usual; his hair fell in tufts behind his ears. He ate his food without salt and realized that his road toward death was ambushed, threatened by the strength of a man who gave solid value to existence. A strange, uncontrollable desire pushed Juan toward Pablo.

Many years ago, when he was still a child, his father had planted a vineyard in the depths of a ravine behind the forest. Juan went down to it one afternoon, fleeing from his thoughts. He wanted his brother's strength, his mistaken, unswerving strength. He longed to see how Pablo advanced without bending, he, Juan Medinao, who always went lurking around corners and among the trees. With a primitive sort of hatred, he would have seized Pablo's faith, his innocence, his freedom. He wanted to absorb all of his security, and even that ignorance, which made his brother go through life so assuredly.

In the ravine, the vineyard was a cemetery of vines. On the ground, wet, slimy grape leaves made him slip. The cold always killed the fruit of that vineyard before it could ripen.

Then he saw a man and a woman gathering vines for kindling. They were Agustín Zácaro and Salome. When they saw him, they stood still like beaten dogs.

Juan approached them, his hair blowing in the wind. "Salome," he said, "your son is a villain."

She lowered her head.

"You all used to live in peace with me. He's hurting the entire village."

Then he realized that his heart was beating hard because Salome looked like her son. She had the same short nose and dark lips. A lock of black, curly hair fell over her brow. He looked away, with trembling hands.

"Master, I can do nothing . . . Pablo is not like us, he's not like anybody. He would allow the devil to take him before giving up!"

"Well, let the devil take him and make ashes of him!" shouted Juan, his face flushed in anger.

"He's not like anybody. He's not like anybody. He's like an angel," whispered voices in his ear.

"Agustín," he finally said. "Warn the people that I will wait until the first of October. If they haven't shown up for work by then, all my land will dry up under the sun. Point out to them, Zácaro, that I don't need you. You, on the other hand, need me."

He turned around and went off.

The men returned to work, and Juan went out to his patio to tell them that he held no grudge against them and that he was happy that they had returned to work his land. Immediately he saw Salome, standing between Agustín and Rosa. But everyone was quiet, and their silence weighed like lead. They went with their plows and yokes toward the abandoned fields.

He looked for Pablo among the field hands to no avail. Like a hungry dog, he sought him in the furrows. He himself picked up a plow and began to work the soil. There ahead, a flock of black birds plunged into the forest. Salome was at his side. The plow was very heavy, and large blisters came out on his hands. His heart fell, like the seed. It grew dark. The bright red soil opened up in violent contrast to the steel-colored sky. In the distance stood trees, hard and black, wounding him with their evocation of his brother.

Juan could no longer contain himself. After spending the day among the peasants, he approached Salome. She raised her eyes to him. How could he have ever thought that she looked like Pablo? In her pupils there was no red transparency of black grapes. She stared at him dumbly with the liquid eyes of a cow.

"Where is he?"

"Who?" It was Pablo's mother, and she was asking him. He could have slapped her.

"Where is your son?"

"Ay, he will never forgive us for having returned to work!" She seemed tired, worn out. She sat down on a rock, her dirty hands on her waist and her head tilted to the side. There was a contained tenderness in her throat; she sighed deeply.

"But where. . . ," he demanded, "where is he?"

There was such violence in his question that the woman just

looked at him silently. "He's just a boy, master. Don't be angry with him."

"What do you know, you dumb beast?" he thought to himself. He turned his back on her, and like a man possessed, he plunged into the woods. The afternoon was coming to an end. There was a subtle, bluish mist in the air. The fallen leaves on the forest floor looked like scattered fire. He asked the game warden if he had seen Pablo go by.

"Yes, he went to the hut that he built in the ravine."

Just as he had supposed. Juan Medinao arrived there sweating and panting heavily.

"Zácaro!" he called.

Pablo was at the door of the hut. He had lit a fire and was watching the flames. He turned to see him.

"Come on back, man! I forgive you from the bottom of my heart!"

"What is it that you are forgiving me for?" asked Pablo.

"I'm saying that you can return to my fields in the position that you held before. I know that you set them all up to it, that it was your fault. But I don't hold a grudge. I want to see you again in my fields, just like before."

Pablo laughed, in the same way that he had thirteen years ago, on the threshing floor, when he threw the stone at him.

"Good God," said Juan Medinao passionately. "You're such a child . . . Come on back! Return, with everybody else . . ."

Instead of responding, Pablo turned his back on him and began watching the fire again. Juan's eyes thirstily engulfed his head and his shoulders, which were haloed in the orange glow of the flames.

"Come now, don't be such a child! Your mother, and Agustín — everybody has returned."

Then Pablo stood up, turned around, and looked straight at him. Juan Medinao felt like retreating. His brother dominated with the height and strength of his young body. The fire accentuated Pablo's wine-colored eyes. Juan Medinao's mouth was dry. He wanted to jump on him savagely and bite his neck, to sink his teeth in slowly,

68

drawing out the pain, and to suck that voice that poured out so clearly: "I have no intention of returning to your land, Juan Medinao. I can't go and mix with those who have gone back to work for you."

"Why do you hate them? Haven't you learned that it is beautiful to forgive."

"I don't hate them. I just can't live among them anymore, as I couldn't live, for example, at the bottom of a river. There is nothing left for me to do in this village, and I will leave as soon as I can. Don't worry anymore about me, Juan Medinao. I don't hate you either. Not you, not anybody. I can't hate or love in the same way you do. Everything is simpler and easier for me."

Juan clenched his teeth. The landscape turned red. Pablo's wine-colored eyes seemed to swirl inside his own eyes, making him drunk with their strength. He could have killed Pablo then and there, chopping him down with an ax like a tree, trampling him underfoot until he fell down exhausted.

"Son of a whore!" he screamed hoarsely. But that insult meant nothing to Pablo. Quietly, he put more kindling on the fire.

"Where do you think you're going to go, you stupid peasant? What do you think you're going to do? You were born to work the soil with your face to the ground. Do you even know what you are and what you want?"

"Yes, I know," calmly responded the boy. "And I also know what you are."

Juan made a noiseless laugh: "Tell me, then."

Pablo, who was breaking up small pieces of kindling, threw them into the fire.

"I am a man: nothing more and nothing less. I want to have time to live, and I want others to have that too. I wasn't born to work the soil. What I would like to do is build houses. Ever since I was a child, I have been thinking about this, and since I haven't been able to study, I will be a mason. Yes, I'd like that. I also want to see everything that exists on this earth and discover what other men do and think. I don't know what you mean when you name a father or a brother. I respect all men and love them in the same way. I want to go places, eat when I'm hungry, and sleep when I'm tired. I want to build my house where I like and have the woman I want. And, when I'm certain that my son can have all of this, I will want a son as well."

"But you're going to die, you miserable fool! You're going to die! Don't you realize that? Time swallows everything; we're just apprentices of death. In the end, you're going to disintegrate in the earth. Then where will all your houses and sons end up? What purpose will your houses and sons serve. . . ?"

"There is no death for me. As long as I am alive, death does not exist."

"You know nothing! You're just a poor, stupid child. You think only about where you've come from and where you're going; you don't even know what it's like to live in a continual fire, with God inside of you. Think about God!"

"I don't know what God is. Nothing exists before or after me. There is no death. I'm on earth, and I like living on earth. I only wish that everybody could share my happiness."

"You! What do you know about happiness? I know what it's like to burn in life, like this forest is now burning. I know fear, love, and suffering. I know, I know. . . !"

Pablo looked at him for a long while. Then, he said: "I told you that I knew what you were, and now I'm going to tell you. I've watched you grow up over me. I've seen how you walked among us. When you were fifteen and wanted a woman, instead of earning her love, you ran off and masturbated. When they hit you and insulted you, instead of defending yourself, you prayed, and cried, and ran away. When you hate, since you can't kill, you forgive. You have money and you save it. I can't hate you in the same way that you hate: I only know that my body rejects you because you're rotten. You don't do anything. You have no purpose in life, not even to build walls

70

for houses. And about that other life that you talk about, supposing that it does exist, do you really think that you will be given it just because you've waited for it, just for having dragged out your long wait here on earth? Wrong, Juan Medinao. You're nobody. You're nothing."

Juan Medinao drew back toward the trees. Damn! Damn! Pablo had crushed the most hidden part of his heart. He had named things that he thought were nameless. At the same time, Pablo remained quiet, kind, innocent. With an enviable faith, clean of the beyond, so different from his own dark, burnt faith.

"I'm your brother, Pablo." His voice sounded like an ancient hidden river, dragging its current toward the depths.

"No more than all men," responded Pablo. Then he entered the hut.

At that moment, Juan became aware of his love. His love, like a tumor, that Pablo would never feel or understand. A love beyond everything and everybody, like a scourge of God. He ran from there because he knew that if he stayed he would drag himself into the hut to beg him like a dog not to leave, to stay at his side. He would ask him never to abandon him or go away, like everything else. Oh, if he could only overcome his brother and be one with him!

Juan went home. Now he understood that Pablo was part of him. He was like the empty shell of his brother, and he needed him and desired his contents beyond all reason.

The mastiff that Juan Senior had bought from Pablo thirteen years before was in the patio. Juan Medinao went to the stable and looked for a rope. He tied it around the dog's neck, and from the other end of the taut line, with his feet sunk in the dust, he watched how the animal, stupidly defenseless, with the slipknot around his neck, strangled himself. A thick slobber stained the ground. He could not even howl, and only a red froth fell over his tongue and through his jaws. When the dog was dead, Juan removed the rope from his neck and ordered the servants to bury him far away.

By the following day, Pablo Zácaro had already left for Central Artámila. Juan found out that he was working there as a farmhand until he earned enough money to go to the city.

Juan Medinao went down to the Zácaros' hut. "I want everybody to know that he's my brother. I want to have him at my side, in my house. I want to share my inheritance with him. Tell me, Salome, how can I make your son return? You're his mother; you know more about him than I do. You know what might bring him back to me and make him accept what I want to give him."

He was sitting in the same kitchen where Rosa had washed the blood from his knees years ago. Salome looked at him with the eyes of a grateful dog. Her astonishment left her speechless. Suddenly she began to shed tears: "You're a good man, master. Better than your father. Better than my son."

"He's my brother," he repeated obsessively. That which he had kept silent for so long now burst from his lips like a burning flower. "He's my brother."

He pressed Salome with questions that overwhelmed her. Juan Medinao knew that Pablo would never betray himself. For that reason, he could not make him the offer directly. Something else would have to attract him to return, otherwise he would never come.

Every night he returned to the Zácaros' hut, with his indomitable hope. Dazzled by Juan's sudden, incomprehensible interest in them, they gave him the best spot by the fire. Agustín watched him silently, with resentment. Rosa showed him the same face of indifference that she had worn when she washed his knees and ordered him to leave the hut. Now she wore a dark expression on her wrinkled face. She listened to them talk and said nothing. One night, in a few words, she said much more than all of Salome's confused and grateful chatter.

"Since he was a child, Pablo has been in love with one of the Corvo girls. I know him well, and I'm certain that he won't go to the city without taking her with him, because she loves him. Sometimes I see her taking the road up to Central Artámila, and I could swear that he comes down to meet her on the road."

The Corvos were the offspring of that old shepherd who owed nothing to the Juans. None of them worked for Juan Medinao. They were one of the few independent families of Lower Artámila. Juan Medinao stood up suddenly and left the hut.

Since his mother and his companions went back to work for Juan Medinao, Pablo had not spoken with any of the laborers. He left the village without even seeing Salome. Juan had been unsuccessfully trying to find some force powerful enough to bring him back. Now, just when he had found him, his brother was getting away. But Juan would make him come back! He would force Pablo to return so that he could bury him at his side, enclosed within the walls of the dark red house, so that he might drink all of his cold purity. His brother and he should be one. They were really a single man. Their separation was painful, as cruel as when the soul abandons the body. He must win Pablo over, capture him, and not let him get away. He could not remain as he was, incomplete, split in two.

Around that time, the people from Central Artámila were celebrating their festival. That afternoon, Juan Medinao saw a girl from Lower Artámila going up the main road. She was blond, thin, and was wearing a green dress. He was certain that she was the granddaughter of the old shepherd Corvo and was on her way to the celebration to meet Pablo Zácaro.

Juan approached to watch her, hiding behind the trees along the road. She had Pablo. She knew the pressure of his body, the salt of his teeth, and his soaked hair. Perhaps she still wore on her skin Pablo Zácaro's scent. Undoubtedly they shared memories and loved life equally. Pablo had certainly instilled in her his devotion to the land, his happiness in concrete and palpable things. Death and God probably did not exist for her either. As Juan dimly understood it, they were clean and young and lived with no anxiety.

He clenched his teeth to keep from calling her and asking about

Pablo. Instead he set off toward the Northwest Cemetery. There, in the graveyard, the grass was greener. Looking through the iron gate, he saw a dog sniffing among the fallen crosses. He threw a rock at the dog, which ran off with something between its teeth. Juan searched for his parents' grave. "While I'm alive, death doesn't exist," Pablo had said. "While I'm alive." How could he ignore bodies reduced to dust? Was he unaware of absences? So many absences, haunting the darkness, floating around us like burnt-out lights.

Without his noticing it, the afternoon came to an end while he was there. A cruel wind brought the smell of mold and wet graves to his nostrils. He turned and quickly returned to his house. Entering the stable, he looked at the horse. The day was approaching when they would bring the wild horses down from the sierra. Twenty colts, black, brown, and gray, would tear down the slope in a wild herd, raising furious clouds of dirt. He shivered. He called the stableboy to saddle up the horse.

As he galloped toward Central Artámila, it was already dark. When he finally made out the village, the sky was black. In the silence of the road, the hooves sounded like the puppeteer's drum. The hooves were blue in the dark. He went at full speed, the wind cutting his face.

At a bend in the road, embraced by the mountains, lay Central Artámila. An unusual radiance arose in the night. Since they were celebrating the festival, there were lights in the main plaza. Unexpectedly the bells began to toll. Bells. A warm trembling traveled through his blood. The deep bells, slow and grave, made a peculiar duet with the drumbeat of the horse's hooves. It was cold, and nevertheless, he was beginning to sweat. Church bells calling to vespers. Lofty bells, not party bells. Their beauty almost hurt him.

The houses of Central Artámila clustered together in the darkness. It was a night without stars or moonlight. The streets were narrow and steep. The horseshoes slipped on the paving stones, making green sparks. He dismounted, tied his horse to a post, and went

74

down an alley that descended darkly to the plaza. Before reaching the corner, he stopped. The walls on either side of the narrow street were so close together that within their confines he could see only a little booth selling candy and paper hats, bathed in the light of the plaza. The wind carried away the sounds from the festival so he could hear nothing. For a while, he seemed to be watching a silent pantomime. Pieces of colorful paper, swinging in the wind, hung from the candy stand's awning. A child, with his back toward him, was handing a coin to the man in the booth. A red paper hat crept over the ground. He felt then as if the wind had entered through his eyes and blown about streamers and colored papers inside him. Within his chest fluttered all of the withered carnival of his birth. He advanced to the end of the street, and after entering the plaza, he stood still. All at once, the music hit him. It seemed that it wasn't he who had turned the corner, but rather that the whole plaza, like an enormous revolving stage, was turning toward him. The center of the plaza was farther down; it was square and three times larger than that of Lower Artámila. He would have to descend stone steps to get there. Below, everybody was crushed together around the band, with many-colored hats and masks. The wind blew countless little paper flags, green and purple. Yellow dust whirled among them. There was something brutal and sordid in the atmosphere, something almost sinister. The musicians, already half-drunk, wore checkered jackets. Beyond, only the little candy stand seemed isolated and fragile, with the air of a dead child about it.

The arched tavern door looked like the mouth of an oven. Juan Medinao headed toward it. Inside, everything was crimson. The men's coarse faces, inflamed, pressed together as they sang over their wine. He noticed the arms and teeth of the woman who served the pitchers. Red wine trickled between her fingers. Juan Medinao entered, and heat plastered his skin. Thick tobacco smoke filled the air. He swallowed the wine, which burned his throat, wiped his face with his forearm and felt that his lips might singe the skin on his arm.

At that moment, anything could have ignited inside him, even green wood.

Then he saw them in a corner. He clung to the wall, beside a curtain edged with faded pompons. They were seated next to a barrel that served as a table and were drinking from the same pitcher. Pablo Zácaro's hair twisted in thick black curls that fell over his eyes. She was wearing a necklace of green glass beads, which sparkled in the light. They wrapped their arms around each other's waist and seemed far from those around them. Juan Medinao paid and left.

Outside the tavern, he spied on them until they came out a short while later. They did not join the others in merrymaking. Instead, they headed off toward the fields, toward the countryside that lay like a green-and-red patchwork quilt behind the houses. The countryside would greet them with its memory of springtime and honeysuckle. It was October, and the ground was damp and covered with rotting leaves, but they carried the sun with them. They had no need of the colored paper or the vulgar music from the plaza. Wherever they went, they took with them the celebration of their lean young years, without serenades filled with memories or portents, and devoured the minutes like stars. Juan Medinao watched them go toward the grass and water, toward the oak trees and wild saffron crocuses. And he remained riveted to the wall, feeling uglier and more knock-kneed than ever.

Juan leapt onto his horse like an attacking wolf. With the same thirst he had brought with him, he galloped home to his village.

On the following day, he went beyond the laborers' huts to the river. Among the reeds, he found Pablo Zácaro's girl. She was washing, with her hands shivering in the cold water. Her bright blue eyes were close together; her hair shone palely in the morning sun. To Juan she looked too thin, though her shoulders were shapely and her breast trembled like that of a dove. Her skin was pale since she did not work under the burning sun in Juan Medinao's fields. Instead she took care of domestic chores. The night before, she had

76

been with him, with Pablo Zácaro, absorbing his breath, his smell of wheat.

"Come here," Juan said. The girl looked up at him in surprise. She then grew frightened by the look in his eyes. He approached her on his twisted legs, his head bent down over her. She took off running, like a startled young doe, awkward and tender. Her wet arms splattered a trickle of bright drops on the ground behind her as she raced toward her house. Obsessed, Juan Medinao followed her. She entered the house and slammed the door shut. Juan began to beat on the wooden door brutally. A great silence hung in the air since everyone had gone to work in the fields. Nobody answered his knocks. Juan called the girl a few times. Then, over his head, he heard the window being shut hastily.

Juan Medinao let his arms fall and slowly went back home.

But now he knew what he was going to do. Anything seemed sensible to him if it would put an end to that absence. Anything rather than relinquish his brother; the separation was driving him mad. He felt as if he were on fire, completely separate from other men. Suffering the pain of a man split in half, like an old hollow oak tree. He was only the bark with ant and spider trails, with wind and moss over his wound.

Two days later, in the evening, when he figured that the Corvos would be at home, he went toward the village. Earlier, he had brought presents from Central Artámila. He knocked at the door, and they opened it. When they saw who it was, the mother and brothers stood quiet, staring at him. The father was eating, with his back to him. Suddenly, without even sitting down, he announced that he was twenty-three years old and had decided to get married. He had seen the youngest Corvo girl and had fallen in love with her. The Bible even said: "It is not good for a man to be alone." He ran his hand through his hair and stood quietly, waiting.

The Corvos remained in silence. The father turned around to look at him. His large square jaws had stopped chewing. The youngest Corvo girl was sixteen. She was half-hidden behind the door, with her simple eyes, not knowing what to do with her hands. As in a story, Juan Medinao asked: "Would you marry me?"

She shook her head and ran upstairs. Juan Medinao opened the packages before the silent Corvo family. On the table he left some colored handkerchiefs, a copper necklace, and a mother-of-pearl rosary. As he went toward the door, the mother hurriedly ran to open it.

"She will live in the big house and will have everything that she needs," Juan said. "She won't have to work in the house or in the fields. Think about it tonight, and tomorrow at this same time, I will return."

On the following evening, when he came in, the Corvos offered him a seat. They called the girl, whose name was Delia. The mother spoke and said that they were all in agreement. Only if grandfather Corvo were still alive, he would have been against it. But now he was in the ground of the Northwest Cemetery. Delia's eyes were bloodshot. He looked at her in silence, and to him she looked simple, tender, and pale, like springtime fruit. Wearing a doelike, timid expression, she tried to escape out the door to the countryside. But the mother grabbed her wrist. When Delia began to struggle, her mother slapped her. Five red marks appeared on her cheek.

"Stay and talk with him," said the mother. The Corvos left the room in silence. And they were left alone.

Delia began to cry like a child. Juan drew her to him without tenderness. He felt her wet face close to his. On her blond eyelashes sparkled tears.

Juan explained: "He loves you and he'll come looking for you. I'll take you to my house, so he will come to my house too." When he bent to kiss her, his mouth filled with all the salt, with all the scent of his brother. Pablo's mouth had also kissed those lips, and they were still wet from her night with him. A wave of blood blinded him, and he furiously bit until he heard her moan. Shoving her away, he left

78

the house without shutting the door. The open door banged against the wall, and a whirlwind of dust and leaves invaded the room. A dog was crossing the plaza, its tongue hanging out.

He galloped his horse to Central Artámila in search of the parish priest. The days sped by quickly, and one morning that seemed the following day, they were married in the parish church and they heard the bells.

He did not see his brother anywhere, even though he had sent Salome to look for him with the news.

When the wedding party returned again to Lower Artámila, the day laborers offered their presents of painted nuts and winter fruit. A strong odor of apples filled the patio. Juan Medinao forbade music and distributed copper coins among the children. The bride entered the house of the Juans looking from side to side as if she were being pursued. In Juan Medinao's stark bedroom no changes had been made. The somber black cross that hung over the bed seemed to fall on the girl's chest. Delia stood quietly in the middle of the room, in her black dress and black mantilla. A bird with swept-back wings flew by the window.

Juan Medinao turned around suddenly and went downstairs. In the empty patio Salome was waiting for him. Upon seeing her, he felt his heart tremble. It seemed to him that he had just entered the realm of shadows and wind. Salome's head hung in defeat; her shoes were muddy from the road.

"Have you seen him?"

She nodded. Then Juan grabbed her by the wrists and dragged her to the columns on the edge of the patio.

"Tell me, woman," he said, squeezing Salome's wrists as if with iron tongs.

She explained how she had gone to look for him. She had told him about the wedding. Pablo, then, had become quiet and thoughtful. Her heart broke as it did when he was little and she saw him step on glass with his bare feet. She had wanted to kiss him. She was sure that Pablo's heart felt cold. He had loved Delia Corvo for so long. . . ! But Pablo had only said: "She can do what she likes."

"But don't you love her?" she had insisted sorrowfully. "Are you going to leave her in the arms of another man? Juan Medinao wants to have you as a brother, in his house. Go with him, and that way you will have her as well." Everything was so simple, but Pablo refused with a distant smile.

"No," he exclaimed with gentle firmness. "If she has married him, I shouldn't interfere in their life. She has done so because it suited her. If it had been the other way around, if I had been the first to leave, I wouldn't want to have her chasing after me like a dog. Everything is fine as it is. Now I don't have to put off going to the city because, if I'm going alone, I can go right now with my hands in my pockets."

This was exactly what had been said. Salome then had left her son alone.

Juan Medinao stood quietly for a while. It was as if there were tiny bursts of laughter all around him, just like little souls floating about his motionless body. He remembered the small, slender black figure that stood alone in the middle of his bedroom, her shadow reaching to the door. His shrill cry broke the silence. Abruptly he headed toward the gate and then out into the countryside. He was running, dazed and feverish, out beyond the huts and the forest. A bitter wind blew against his sweating body. Autumn had left the landscape bare.

He reached the bottom of the ravine. The vineyard lay in silence, lifeless. The blood-red sun was sinking behind the forest. Burdened with sorrow, he felt the physical pain of a mutilated man whose wounds were covered in salt. Pablo was not there. Pablo had fled. But it made no difference anymore, because even if he did have him at his side, in his house, entombed in his life, he understood that Pablo would always be outside him, outside his body and soul, far from his blood and spirit. Juan Medinao was a man condemned to emptiness, to absence.

Then it was that he saw Salome. She was among the vines and the fallen leaves, crying. Over their heads they heard a noise approaching and growing louder. It was a repetitive rumble, full of reverberations. Juan Medinao shuddered. Thundering down the slope came a herd of wild horses, manes in the wind, in a furious cloud of copper-colored dust. The horse driver let out a long, very long cry that died away over the naked trees. A rain of rocks rolled down the slope, bounding toward the river. Whinnies pierced the afternoon air, and the drumbeat of the hooves echoed in Juan's racing blood. He was plunged into deep desperation that ground him into the earth like a dead man. The burning dust stirred up by the herd entered his eyes and ears, his nose and mouth. Juan Medinao looked at Salome through the fiery cloud of dust. With her eyelashes lowered to protect her eyes, she looked like Pablo. Her nostrils trembled almost imperceptibly. Her lips were firm, and her skin shone as if polished by walnut juice. Her teeth, knife-sharp. If she did not raise her eyelids, one could believe that her eyes were full of his wine, of his impossible, dark red wine. She was so close, with her shining black ringlets tickling his face. He bit her neck, her round chin, desperately grasping at empty reasons. Her scent of apples and wheat filled him with emotions of absence and impossibility. Panting like a lion, he knocked her down onto the slimy yellow leaves. The horses' hooves were now in his veins, in his eyes. They were crossing the river, slipping on moss and stones. A rain of mud fell upon them, along with the agonizing shout of the horse driver. The hoofbeats disappeared in the distance. They disappeared like everything, like everyone.

"And now for the present, Father, since I'm getting old, my principal sins are gluttony and laziness."

Juan Medinao had finished his confession. The young priest gave him absolution with his waxen hand. On the following day he could take Holy Communion and listen to the bells.

8

The burial site was ready. The mother, at the door of the hut, begged the doctor not to mangle her child. The old man shoved her aside. The smashed-up corpse was beginning to rot. The stench filled the room and steamed up the windowpanes. Pedro Cruz, his face ashen, held his beret in his hands.

The old doctor lit up a crumpled cigar and began to swear at the ribbons and paper flowers that covered the body. He started to rip them off, slashing them with his knife. The naked wound appeared then, all shriveled up. The black-and-blue fingernails stood out grotesquely on the lemon-yellow hands of the corpse. But what hurt his mother most was to see his head, covered with black curls, as it knocked against the floor while the doctor worked on the body.

"But, woman, he can't feel anything now. . . ," Pedro Cruz told her desperately, in response to her screams.

"What do you know?" she said, biting her handkerchief.

The young priest, with his eyes closed, began to recite prayers for the dead. From the shadow, Juan Medinao watched closely.

Outside, the village children waited impatiently in small groups, as they would at the door of a baptism. They stamped their feet in the cold, and two of them were rolling in the mud, wrestling and laughing. Before the body was brought out, the neighboring women had placed the artificial flowers in his mouth once again. The children lined up. One or two still carried scraps from Dingo's wagon, like war trophies. Juan Medinao presided over the procession along with Pedro Cruz. Dingo no longer remembered those childish times. Dingo had already forgotten. How can men forget? He, now, behind Pedro Cruz's son, relived his mother's burial. They were the same voices, the same steps, the same celebration in the Northwest Cemetery.

At the graveyard, a group of children had climbed up on the wall and paraded in masks they had found in the puppeteer's trunk. Pedro Cruz shouted at the children and dispersed them by throwing stones. "I'll get you, I'll. . . ," he howled. And he shed a tear because he had no more children at home. The sun placed a halo around three cats that sat on the wall like little saints. The black book trembled in the young priest's hands. The doctor took a sandwich out of his pocket and began to chew it with his false teeth, which came loose after each bite. They put the child in a wooden box and nailed down the cover with some difficulty since they could not cross his arms. The doctor wiped his mouth with his handkerchief and then began to dig between his teeth and gums with his little finger. The young priest now prayed "Gloria. . . ," for Pedro Cruz's son was not yet seven years old.

It was customary to throw dirt on the coffin once it was in the grave. But the new priest was not used to this practice and could not avoid a startled jump backward before the avalanche of children, who, with savage joy, began to grab up clumps of dirt and throw them. Rocks also fell, making a dull thud as they hit the wood. Nor was Pedro Cruz aware of this custom, since he had spent his life in the mountains. Again he shouted: "I'll get you, I'll . . ." Then, head bowed, he turned abruptly and ran from his son's burial. Out through the graveyard gate he ran like a wild man. The women turned to watch him. "Gloria" was repeated in the prayers, like a puff

83

of wind. The ceremony was still not finished when Pedro Cruz and his flock began clambering up the mountain in a cloud of yellow dust.

The village children set to straightening the fallen crosses, in hopes that the young priest would give them some coins. The old doctor took out his pad and began to write up the record of the autopsy.

In the European Women Writers series: